Looking for a wave

J. M. Couper
Looking for a wave

BRADBURY PRESS SCARSDALE, NY

Library of Congress Catalog Card Number: 75-11112. Printed in the United States of America. First American edition published by Bradbury Press, Inc. 1975. ISBN: 0-87888-085-2.
5 4 3 2 1   79 78 77 76 75
The text of this book is set in 11 pt. Janson.

Looking for a wave

1

Dear Mark,

Have been reminded by my dutiful husband to write you and let you know about the position of the toaster you gave us for our wedding. First of all thank you for such a great gift, but as George has told you we already have one and so if it is quite okay by you, we would like to have it changed.

Enclosed is a photo of an Electric Portable Hand Mixer which sells for the same price as a $50 toaster. If on your inquiries about same, the cost is more than you wish then we are quite willing to trot out the difference. It is something I do want, Mark, so please let me know if you would have any trouble, etc. The toaster at the moment is at Mr. and Mrs. Paton's place, if it isn't any trouble to get it from there. I have told Mrs. Paton about the situation and that it may be changed for another gift.

When you do fix this arrangement it might be as well to leave it with the Patons and when next we are in Sydney we could pick it up then. This would save you any more inconvenience that we may have caused you.

Anyway, thanks for being best man. We were so pleased that you made the wedding and from what I can remember you seemed to enjoy it as did everyone else.

Once again thank you for the trouble of changing the toaster for an Electric Hand Mixer.

Regards,
JANEY MOLYNEUX

P.S.   George sends his best wishes.

The letter was folded to look as chic as a Christmas card, with a bunch of dinky flowers on the front. It was designed for inarticulate people with only one thing to say. On the back at the foot it said NOTELET in very large letters. Mark examined it distastefully, as though it were an unwanted baby in need of a wash. His nose curled. "Well, BLOODY HELL," he said, in block capitals. And he felt this very pressing need to scratch his leg with frightful energy.

You can't tell what your friends are made of, can you? he said to himself.

George Molyneux was a really old-aged friend from school, and here he was sending his best wishes, second-hand. It was a thing you couldn't do unless you didn't give a damn for a person at all, and could live without him perfectly well. So much for being best man at his wedding, hiring a dress suit, holding the ring and all, reading out those telegrams as if you cared. Made you feel like a used contraceptive, or a public convenience. It was a huge indignity, but there wasn't any use going on about it. They'd had to get married, and here was his wife Janey showing no more finesse in writing letters than she had in making love. Maybe you were better without your friends once they were married? It saved you having to endure their wives.

Yet for the minute, with this NOTELET in hand, Mark was sorry he didn't have a wife himself, just to answer for him. But the crisis passed and left him single.

He tried to pretend he'd gained a toaster. But, no, she couldn't stay married without that (what was it?) Electric Portable Hand Mixer. Ah, well, George could buy it for her.

God help his old friend George. Poor George.

2

Later on, Mark was ashamed of himself. It was rough to think in that way, even if only to yourself, even if Janey's letter was sublime in its selfishness.

Well, he said to himself, you're a toaster to the good. Go north, young man.

He'd been meaning to go north. You can spend the summer in New South Wales just looking for a wave. Which is better than looking for a parking spot in the city, any day, and you find a wave oftener. He was a student and his years of traveling to the university had aged him considerably. Trains full of intensive men in the morning, as serious as their pork pie hats, staring at the lists on the Stock Exchange: and in the evening with their minds bedraggled taking a stern eyeful of the sex in the very latest papers, with the very latest, tired advertisements. And then they all go home and sit silent at dinner among a pack of strangers, as if they were still in the train. He vowed he would have none of it. As soon as he was done, he'd be off. All those sad people. Especially as there was sure to be a thigh-load of sex in the train car beside them all, dressed like a circus, laughing at their pork pie hats. A pretty girl was a thing you could at least be a cheerful hypocrite about, surely. You couldn't, for God's sake, really prefer the figures on the Stock Exchange? Besides, he liked fresh air.

So there was this terrific way to live, all summer. You took your exams, and about the end of November you smelled out the Pacific Highway, and made off. Mark was on a Teachers' College Scholarship, and the students who have them are always miserably poor. They think the scholarship sould be about doubled; students are very human: they need their gas and smokes and women too, and it takes money. Mark was looking for only one of these, and on the cheap even then. If you had to go bankrupt to amuse a woman, you couldn't be much fun for her yourself. It was a good rule, he thought, and it made for solvency. That was how he had enough to keep him more or less, while the summer was there for spending. After all, just to be twenty years old is to be fairly well-to-do.

Taking a pal with you? he said to himself. Well, a queer thing and maybe our thoughts do us no credit, but a fellow by the name of Sparrow came into his head then. Sparrow and he had never been mates, but they both played on the Uni golf team and in the past May in the Inter-Varsity they'd been at Newcastle together. Sparrow and his two mates were broke before they started, and they knew who to touch for money, and Mark had never seen it again. Three fives = $15. Now the three of them would flop beside him intimately on the campus and tell him things he had no right to know, as if he'd bought their private lives. And they were looking at Mark, and not Mark at them. It was okay if they fleeced you, and you were a mean little bastard for keeping on thinking about it and hoping for your money back. You ought to feel bloody ashamed. Mark did.

But he wasn't taking anybody hitched to him up the highway. He'd make his friends as he went.

All that kind of planning was pretty good fun while the exams were on and protected him from any sudden action, but, through carelessness on his part, one morning he found

4

himself slap up against a lot of empty good weather, with no exams to distract his attention. To stave off the fine day, he thought he'd make for this garage where Yvonne tickled all the truck drivers. He had this sneaking feeling that he might be kidding himself about this venture. For it's a very real thing to do, takes courage, to shed the rest of your life just like that and set off up the Pacific Highway looking for a wave. The Pacific Highway carries right on to Cairns, and what if you didn't find one till then? Or even if you kept on finding waves one after another till you found yourself in Cairns? Cairns was all of two thousand miles from where Mark was standing teetering with decision on the very verge of Sydney. Maybe Sydney wasn't such a bad spot after all. And if you got to Cairns, they'd only tell you: Carry on, boy — on to Cape York! People weren't all that kind. And you could get enough of waves.

Oh, Lord, in spite of everything, there he was messing about. It was a thing he was prone to, a tenderness against doing anything, as if he were a committee, or even just one of those eternal bastards tootling and tootling over the roads in cars. It isn't doing anything, mostly. Just rubberized modern life, that's all. Surrounded by that, Yvonne and her garage kept receding into the haze of hopeless places.

Desperately, Mark grabbed his savings bankbook and stuffed it into his pocket and shouted, "So long, Mum." He was still in his bedroom looking at himself in the mirror and he hadn't much idea of where his mum was. It was all right, she was sure to come running. He was wondering whether shorts were a fit place for a bankbook. No, he thought, shorts were meant for backsides and no more. A bankbook needs a bit of ballast.

Jeans, he thought, and started rummaging.

Mum had come in, and now he'd have to say "So long" face to face, and he hated that. It was what you got for thinking ahead. Now he might have to stay at home just to save himself embarrassment.

"Where you off to?" Mum said, severely, finding him with one leg half into his jeans. She didn't approve of raw family life. She didn't think it necessary to shout "So long" every time you dived into your jeans. Dancing attention on her son Mark and on her hopes for him, she's given him up many times. Now here he was at home, getting up late and bothering her. Three whole months of that. Why couldn't he get a job?

"I'm thinking of going up the highway for a spell, Mum. As far as Taree. Hitching. Looking for a wave."

"Oh," she said, feeling lighter. She's heard it all, though, before. "You can't go too soon for me," she said, goaded by his rump, which turned blue, and was stuffed with bankbook. There was something disgustingly brazen about jeans. They seemed to take on a boy's muscles, or a girl's. Mum dodged, fastened her disapproval on the shorts in the middle of the floor, bent and picked them up.

"Do you have to lift those? Oven-fresh?" Mark enjoyed teasing her, to the point of offence. "I'll take a toothbrush, and soap, and a razor. I'll take these shorts, too, and maybe—"

"So long as you get going," Mum said. "I don't mind clearing up if you're out of the way, not—"

"Yes, well. So long, Mum," said Mark, kissing her a foot from her cheek, squeezing her arm for good measure. Severe like that, she wouldn't have wanted anything more touching.

"I'll write. Don't worry. It'll give you a break. Thanks for everything, all this year. Oh—I've forgotten to get any Christmas presents yet, but there's—I'll—"

"Be off with you," Mum said. "Always dithering. Such a fuss."

6

"Dad okayed the trip, often, didn't he?"
"You know what he told you. What he said was—"
"Yes, I know. So long."

3

Gingerly, Mark approached the garage, rectangular with ugliness. Places like that could make anybody tentative, buildings of a meaningless utility, like toilets. It was hell for the eye to look on and you asked for fuel quick. Mark was grateful to this service station because they hadn't thought of streamers yet, to fight it out with the sky.

And then there was Yvonne at this garage.

"Yvonne. I was wondering, any truckies looking for a bit of company going north?"

"Don't get fresh," Yvonne said.

She was having her morning tea, laced with gasoline and oil. Yvonne was a lush blonde, ripe as make-up. She was separated from her husband and she had three kids and she worked at this garage. So when she wanted a holiday from herself, truck drivers were the most convenient thing. She just poured some gas into the last truck, hopped into the cabin, and made off. She got to know the bloke a lot better as the fortnight passed. Mark was puzzled that he couldn't ask her. It wasn't a permissive question. If people were allowed to behave in one way or another, surely you could be allowed to show, without disguise, that you knew which way they behaved. But it didn't seem so. Maybe you had to have your own permissive ticket? That'd be it. Say anything you like, and it's okay, so long as you are permissing yourself.

And Yvonne could see that Mark wasn't. His face still shone and looked happy. He liked Yvonne too, or he wouldn't have asked her about anything, and he was sorry for her left by herself with three children, and with a living body on her, and lonely. Lonely maybe day and night. Life fell like hailstones around about you, and some folks seemed to get it more than most.

"Sorry, Yvonne," he said. "It's just that—the exams are over. And there's George Molyneux my old mate up there at Newcastle. Sends me his best wishes and it's not good enough. Because he's married now to his wife Janey, and—"

"You needn't tell me all his history, I'm busy. And he'll recover. He'll be glad to come back to you any day now. All you men recover."

She emptied her cup, pretending it was tasty, and she clashed it among the slops. She didn't smoke, for a wonder. She was very clean and beautiful and cheerless.

"Oh," said Mark, thinking of anything quickly, "I gave them a toaster."

"Lucky them. Wish I had one."

"Thought I'd look in and tell them they could swop it okay. Got one already."

It suited Yvonne's sad side to talk to the young fellahs that came about the garage. It touched her if they were sorry for her, and then she resented it wildly and let loose all her bitterness on them, and then she was so thankful if they listened. She wanted to reach out and touch their sleeves, only for a moment, because they didn't bar her out of the happiness of life that she'd been robbed of. She looked kindly at Mark, amused at him and his rueful faces about a toaster, about which nobody cared. And then their eyes met and they laughed and were friendly.

8

"You poor boob," Yvonne said. "That's what they think of your gift?"

"Oh, it's a compliment, a ruddy compliment. To ask me and not the other person to do the swop."

"Oh, come off it."

Yvonne began stacking chewing-gum. And then this A40 came in for juice.

"The old biddy," said Yvonne, coming back to the till. "Why don't you try her? Go on."

But Mark just looked at Yvonne, on the defensive. She pressed the buttons impatiently.

"Gutless," she said. "I've always wondered about you. Thirty-four, thirty-six, thirty-eight, forty. All talk, you students, and mostly grouses about nothing." She swept past him. "I'll put you on the spot. Get you out of my hair."

For the next minute, standing at the driving window, keeping the change in her own hand, she went on in an animated way to the old biddy. Mark clutched at his kitbag and kicked it an inch or two under his chair. He felt detached from himself, as if he were watching a killing on TV.

"Give her the change," he muttered, "come on." He picked at the silly little table by his elbow. Here was Yvonne thinking that this old biddy was the shot for him. This one had glasses, very light-colored ones to match her hair that was struck by lightning, too. She kept on blinking like a cow at a gate, ready to see a joke even before it was there. She was looking from Yvonne to Mark and back again, and wiggling her fingers for her change to show that she was as practical and busy as any other woman that came along. When she started fiddling with the gear lever, Yvonne got desperate, flung the change into her hand and shouted,

"Hey, you, Mark. Come and let's get rid of you this minute. This old lady's very kind. Think she might take

9

you. If you'd only," she said, taking a step toward Mark, "be polite enough to come and ask."

"I was telling her about the toaster," said Yvonne lamely, as Mark came straggling out. He was easing his kitbag on his shoulder, but he still meant to say no, or thought he did.

He didn't. In two minutes the A40 was chortling along the highway with Mark staring out through the windshield in a bored way, as if he were playing the knight's part to give old ladies his company, and clutching his kitbag at his knee. Actually, he was suddenly aware that perhaps it was more comfortable at home. Who was he to set out on expeditions all on his own? All right for Yvonne, with a seasoned truckie to squire her. And the old biddy kept on talking and talking, as though she were the one that was under some strain.

"I could see you were a student right away." That meant Yvonne had told her. "Nearly didn't take you on because of that, but you asked so nicely."

"Oh yeah?" said Mark to the windshield. "You thought it would be a big thrill for me, I bet?"

You don't take too kindly to those that give you a hitch. Think they'll patronize you, that's what you do. It's awkward: you have to be careful not to resent them too savagely, or to put them in place by telling them of all the exams you've just passed. And Mark didn't know where the hell he was going yet, how could he?

"Tell me," she said. "All this free love. Is there as much of it as they say?"

"Who say? And how much do they say?"

"Oh, everybody. They all say it goes on."

She looked up sideways, over the edge of her glasses. It was a very progressive look, in its intention, and it irritated Mark.

"You shouldn't be interested in that sort of thing. I'll have to be asking you to let me off. Just in case," Mark said, turning slowly from the windshield to the biddy.

The sharp little eyes were sent back to their work, twinkling over the wheel.

"At your age?" he said.

"Oh, I don't know, I don't know at all. You can't help hearing what they say. And journalists never get tired of it. And the young have a reputation to keep up, now haven't they?"

She pursed her lips and nodded her head, as though she were merely making a point about yesterday's rain. Mark couldn't decide whether it was envy or delight that ran in her veins.

"You aren't going to tell me?" she said.

"Trouble is," said Mark, "I ask all the wrong ones. Haven't got the knack of it, but here's hoping."

"The wrong ones? The right ones? Which are which?"

"It all depends," he said, "what you're up to."

He was edging nearer the door, in case he had to run for his private life at any moment.

"You're really a shy boy," she said, and it didn't help.

"Like most boys, or some, anyway. Oh, after parties," Mark said, "there's always a bit of activity, propositioning, seeing home. And there's all this shacking up."

"Oh, shacking up. Yes, do tell me."

Mark said quickly, "I live at home. With Mum."

They laughed, but it was Mark's laugh that came later, and wobblier. He wasn't at ease. He knew that the things you said to your cronies were supposed to be equally good for the old biddies now, too, but it wasn't how his parents had arranged it. He felt cut short in his experience. It still embarrassed him to talk to old biddies below the navel, and he hoped perhaps it always would.

And yet she looked the most harmless soul in the world.

11

4

By the time they were among the give-away centrifugal bits of Newcastle, things had changed. The biddy, to all appearances, was getting a lift in Mark's car, and while he drove he was comforting her with some of his own spare youth. If she liked, she could be young again by giggling away. And so he told her about the famous golf strip-tease that happened at Newcastle when last he was there. Bashing the brake on, beating the lights, keeping a stern eyeful of all the other jokers jostling for the lanes, he extolled himself to his audience.

"Hadn't I better drive?" asked Biddy, anxiously.

"Like hell," said Mark. "I'm doing all right. Sit and rest your pulse. And I have it in for Newcastle."

"But—"

"No bloody buts about it, you wanted me to drive? Last time I was here you should have seen me. Had them all on their backs. And all I had was a golf club then, not this palatial limousine."

All this rough bouncing over other people and their wishes . . . Even nice young fellows, Biddy noticed for the umpteenth time, have this notion of themselves now, that they've only got to joke about and it becomes politeness. Indecent language, for one thing, was made decent by good humor. As if they said: I know I'm being rude, but because I'm admitting it and having a bit of fun out of it, it's all right, isn't it? She didn't think it was, but then she wasn't clever.

Mark was slapping the leather of the seat in a fleshy way.

"Isn't it funny?" he said. "You soon get affectionate for the cars you drive. Just like wife-swopping, I shouldn't wonder. You find yourself glowing over the change. Don't you think? I only know about cars, yet."

But she was still uneasy, the old biddy. About the traffic, he supposed. Her glasses were sweating a bit. He's have to rally her.

"Fact is," he said, "a golf club was about all I had left in the world that day. Had given away everything else but my youps."

"What's youps?"

He'd thought that would get her in. You could play on those old biddies, and it was therapeutic. Like political violence. You shocked them out of their stodgy and decadent ways. Brightened the world.

"Youps," he said. "Why, U.P.s, of course. U-P-S, youps, underpants. Got it?"

"Gracious me," she said. "Yes, course I got it."

But it wasn't entirely successful and he had to improve on it.

"Thirty-four," he said. "What's yours?"

And then she laughed instead of answering.

He had to shift down for a hill with a smouldering bloody great truck on it. Between golf and gears, getting the old biddy giggling, remembering some brilliant impudence gone by, he was feeling a certain euphoria. It isn't every fellow that has made the headlines by the time he's twenty, even if it's only in the Newcastle daily whatever it's called. And now he was back in town again and they's better look out. NUDE STUDENTS AT ROYAL NEWCASTLE. He hadn't ever shown it to his mum. They're quickly horrified are mums. So here he was hamming it up for the old biddy because she was a stranger. She'd have to take it because it didn't matter.

"We'd won the golf the day before, see. *We* were the great-

13

est. Melbourne, Adelaide, Canberra, all those snooty bastards. They had to take it as we dished it out. You feel a kind of a patriotism coming over you, doing battle with these sods. We won. So we got drunk."

"Oh, is that all?" Biddy cried.

"No. That was only the start."

Biddy subsided into the grimness of listening as quickly as she could. It was her own fault. You only made mistakes with hitchhikers, it seemed.

"Next day after breakfast there was this stroke competition to choose an inter-Varsity team to play the professionals, and why should we need to be chosen again, eh? Tell me that. We'd won, hadn't we? There was this Jack Sparrow and Dowsabel—"

"Who?"

"Dowsabel. His name was Bell. We had this flagon of wine between us, and we soon got behind them all. I tell you what," he said, looking earnestly at Biddy, "drunk or not, we still could hit it out with the soberest screwball among them. Mean, jealous committee bastards, voting themselves in, that's all it was for."

He took a corner a bit fast and he had to accelerate to counteract, and these bucket seats in the A40s, they clash together at a thing like that. Biddy went back into her corner nicely tickled up, Mark thought.

"And those two guys, they took a swig for every extra yard we made. They celebrated anything, even the divots flying. We couldn't putt. The hole went dizzy on us."

"That's enough of this," said Biddy gently.

"Oh no it isn't. Haven't told you yet"

"Let me drive, and you can tell me. I can imagine very well."

"Oh, you don't need to. We started playing for our clothes. Hadn't any money to bet on, see. And on a golf course—"

14

He's shouting a bit, Biddy thought.

"On a golf course you soon run out of bloody clothes. The odd sock, T-shirt, it's all you wear. Soon, for God's sake, here was Dowsabel weighed down with three T-shirts, three pairs of shorts, socks and shoes strung around his neck, now wasn't that funny? Sparrow and me playing naked. Only Dowsabel could see the bloody hole, because he has a glass eye, you would think. Dowsabel like a pawnbroker's shop on the move, Jack Sparrow and I rising from the green sea like Botticelli, or something. Must have been a pretty sight, you reckon? When the boys come marching home, with the breeze behind them, up the eighteenth fairway."

Mark leaned over and a note of gravity crept into his voice again.

"True as I'm telling you," he said, "there was a gallery by the clubhouse and they were all rolling about as if a cyclone had struck them down. Heels laughing above their heads and pale panties bursting into tears, it was the whole Jack and Jill business over again. All of a sudden, too. Vice-Chancellor was there pissing himself. Doesn't happen every day, does it?"

Careless with the elation of having achieved his story, or it might still have gone on—there was this bump and bang. Mark rammed down the brake and cursed himself back into presence of mind.

They'd hit the car in front.

5

The male world, always barging about, always collapsing. And there was this bird in the ruins of a Volksy, weeping. That was all. You couldn't call it a big disaster.

"You—" And then Mark said to himself: she's weeping. "Sorry," he said.

He took his hand off the handle of her door, whirled about on his heel, cursed himself for a bloody noisy bull-merchant, pushed the sky up with his two great fists, but all these signs of energy were nothing but five minutes late. He looked back at Biddy to see how she was taking it, and he even had the cheek to think that now, because she was older, here was her chance to help. But she'd tried to get the wheel back, and he still had to go on with his fool story. He seized the handle of that Volksy again.

"I'm sorry," he said. "I really am. It was my fault. You all right, Biddy?" he called. "Look what I've done to your car. Slosh me one if you like."

In the emergency he called her Biddy, and it stuck. But suddenly that bird stopped weeping and went for him properly. He was grateful, he admired her intensely, agreed with every word she said. You can't keep on apologizing for it bores people to death, and it lets you out to be contrite by just listening. She'd been watching him weaving about in her mirror for a long time. And there was this truck in front. She'd been in a predicament and this was the way she'd got

16

out of it, thanks to him for a bloody great fool. Give her truck drivers any day.

The bumpers had locked on impact, and when she felt it she must have slewed into the side, and Australian roads usually have a kind of supporting desert on either side, far wider than the bitumen, and they had shunted on to that, except for the rear wheel of the A40, and something had set the horn of the Volksy going like a voice crying *Sleep no more*. She really had to shout to give him his character. Even then she refused to scream, talking fast, her hair about her eyes. Mark couldn't help thinking to himself, at least I chose a good-looker. But she was older than he was.

The traffic slowed down a bit as it lambasted along, and they all had a good geek, mums and their kids, truckies, travelers, the lot: mums showing the need for good manners at all times, kids picking their noses and pointing, men grim with somewhere to go. The rest of the world was going by, though they were in the ditch. Mark began to feel protective toward this bird that was ticking him off and it gave her, in his opinion, an extra right to have a go at him. It was almost as if he'd pitched his tent among his women.

". . . not paying the slightest heed to your driving at all. Waving your arms like a demented cop. Saw you in the mirror. Knew you'd better watch out. And you didn't. And can't you stop that bloody horn? This bloody great truck changing down and I had to brake, of course I had to, you should have been watching and I knew you weren't."

She bit her lip and wiped her nose with her forefinger, a thing that girls don't often do unless they trust their company, and she shook her hair about her face and scratched her head and sobbed.

"Where'd I put those tissues, oh hell? Did I ask for this?"

"There, there," Biddy said, "you're right, dear, and safe, and you mustn't take on—"

"Take on? To be snookered like this. I couldn't go any faster and you should have been looking. You'd better call the police. I'm not budging, not a bloody inch." She climbed out of the car.

"I'll get on a phone," said Biddy.

"I'm not budging and if it's a write-off it's all because of your lousy driving and here I am—I can't—I've plenty to do besides bite your ear off. What's the time? Oh, dear! You're all the same you young hoods just buggering everything up."

She looked strangely beautiful swearing, though Mark didn't want her to swear too trenchantly on such a brief acquaintance, and she didn't. Summed him up, that's all.

"Shouldn't be allowed on the road, not at any time. Oh where's—?" She scrambled for that tissue and blew her nose, took a deep breath, felt better, was off again.

"Wouldn't even care, but with a Volksy . . . I'd drive with the rear bashed in, but with a Volksy there's the engine in the back and why did you have to choose me? Why me? Gossiping and going on like a tea party. Waving your arms like a woman hanging clothes. You a man."

She turned her back to him and pushed the Volksy with her thighs, just to be doing something. She had a very fine flat back, that vanished into shapeliness, too.

"Miles from home," she said. "Oh what do I do now? I suppose it's lucky it's Newcastle, a town, at least."

Mark gazed about on the emptiness of many houses, saw Biddy coming back. She was all right, and he was glad of it. The accident was beginning to drag. He still had to apologize to her and see what had happened to the A40: nothing much, he thought, but it was hardly tactful to look and rejoice at that. He raked the ground with his foot, and she took it for contrition.

"You weren't thinking, were you?"

18

"No," he said, "but—Fancy meeting you this way? I mean, meeting anybody interesting—" And his voice petered out and he tried to beg the attention of her eyes and speak to them, a thing more dangerous than driving. With her mouth growing softer and her hair disheveling her face, she had a look about her of contradictory victory. He admired her, and he was glad if maybe she quite liked him, or could, notwithstanding everything. Biddy came up and said she had called the police, and they waited, almost like friends.

The police force came on a motor-bike, revving it up in a wide arc, as though he had all the importance of a jet airplane landing. Up to his job, he promptly dismissed Mark with no notice at all.

"What's on?" he said. "Madam?"

Even before he was off his bike he was edging his shoulder between plaintiff and defendant. And he had to be careful that he wasn't giving the impression of a dog at a lamppost. Finally, when he had escaped this hazard, he stood beside his handlebars and bent his knees with graceless equanimity, getting his bowels in trim.

"What's on? Eh?"

He cocked his head out of sheer politeness. But things had changed since they'd phoned him.

"Oh, constable, it's not so much as I thought. Sorry to trouble you, I feel so confused with this horn going all the time. I wonder, could you—?"

The force went over and looked steadily. But the noise must have got into his ears all at once, for he ripped at something desperately and stopped it. Silence drifted around them like the blessed sunshine. Cars swished by with new noises.

"There's a tow-truck coming," the constable said. "I passed him on the way."

Some constables, they say, nurse their tow-trucks like pilot-fish.

"Laying any charge?" the constable said.

He had his book out and he was busy lifting incriminating details from the registration stickers.

"Oh, no, constable, wouldn't dream of it. Though I was pretty peeved at first and wouldn't you be?"

"Driving licences?" the constable said.

And while he was looking at them, Lin, this girl in the Volksy, ran all her words together and kept the party pleasant in a don't-mind-me sort of way, but when she saw that he was finished and was fit to listen, she said,

"All I want to know is: who pays?"

"Oh, I will," said Mark.

"Thanks," Lin said. "Will you write that down, too, please, constable?"

The force shot her a nervous glance, but she persisted in smiling at him with inflexible approval. He turned on Mark.

"I'm warning you, driver, that anything you say may be used in evidence against you."

"Still," Mark said mildly, "I'll pay."

And Biddy came in then.

"Oh," she said, "the other car's mine, constable."

"But I was driving it," said Mark.

He looked at Mark hard and low and long, and Mark kept up his anxious face, and said no more. The cop recovered his control and fell back on his monosyllabic style.

"Speed?" he said pithily.

"Oh—"

"No more than ten miles an hour," Lin said.

"I might have—"

"Any—"

"—been doing fifteen—"

"—skid marks?"

"—I suppose."

20

"No skid marks," the constable said, answering himself, closing his book and rapping it.

"Heavy wagon," Lin said, "right in front. I had to slow down. This hill."

"We're all good friends, I see," said the force, sarcastically. "I'll be getting on my way. P'raps some other day, young feller. Your luck's in."

He went uphill with a really uproarious noise, and when he was gone,

"Could we have a drink or something?" Mark said.

6

They were sitting in a deli, with Cokes mostly drunk.

"What that policeman saw," Mark said, "was that, for a pack of strangers, and at war, we liked each other."

"Liar," Lin said.

"Well, you two were pretty decent about it, anyway."

But their nerves were too tired for any compliments. Lin took in the other customers and the flies, the sloppy tables, all the artillery of the bar. She turned to Biddy and said,

"A flatterer, that's all he is."

She emptied her glass. All three had been saving the last mouthful, because after that nobody would know what to do next. But now she was off, gathering up her things.

"Oh," said Biddy, "I only met him this morning. He doesn't flatter me. But then, you know, he's attentive. Wanted to give me a rest. I'd say that's why he was driving."

She was warning Lin, somehow.

"I know," said Lin, undecided, flickering a look at Mark. "I suppose he's not always a goat. But I have to go," she said, getting up.

"Look here, Biddy," said Mark. "Do you mind if we call you Biddy? Just among the three of us. Yvonne thought of it first, not me. Look here, this is my bankbook and I mean to pay up. Garage says they'll both be fixed tomorrow late. A40 maybe today. It's not worth bringing the insurance in, is it? Takes months."

Lin sat down again.

You have to pay about half the bill anyhow when you're under twenty-five, and it hampers your youth with unnecessary business. So there was his bankbook on the table.

It wasn't that they ruled the money out, but they both looked at it distastefully. Perhaps there were more fitting places, even though that day they were nowhere. Biddy had lit a cigarette.

"Please put it away," Lin said.

"I've got—"

"Who wants to know?"

"—about plenty, then."

He was puzzled by their attitude, and it made them feel for the moment that he was the one who needed looking after.

"Tell you what," he said. "Where's Kotara? It can't be far away. I was best man to a chap once. Lately, in fact. And I've got to call on him, about a toaster. I feel so nervous, and we've got to do something, while we're waiting. Let's all go?"

"No, thanks," Lin said. "If we go back to the garage, see how they're doing, then maybe we can, well, get rid of each other. Settle up, and take off. I've plenty on my mind without any toaster. We can't let such a thing as a car accident make us bosom friends."

"No, we can't," said Biddy, gently.

She sounded sorry. Biddy had nearly lived past all the friends she had ever made in the world. It was no cause of pleasure to her.

"We've been managing up to now, haven't we?" said Lin to Mark.

"Yes, but when it dawns on you what you've been missing—oh, I mean you grow up. Everything's so casual and glancing by, and how do you stop to speak to somebody: and say anything she might like: or be serious for a minute?"

"Oh—"

"Okay, okay, I was waving my hands about, just like you saw, in your mirror. But I don't always and—"

"Look here," Lin said, "we're not sitting side by side at a show."

"Okay, okay," said Mark, nettled, repeating himself. "We'll go to the garage."

But it still crept back into his mind to go and call on George and Janey. He hadn't wanted to be their best man. He didn't want to swop their toaster. They could do something for him, and entertain his friends. Who could bear to roam around the suburbs of Newcastle, waiting, feeling useless?

Janey and George had taken great pains with the modern world until they seemed built right into it. When George was at Harvard Business School, it just occurred to him one day, now that he was a graduating tycoon, that the next step was a wife. Tender memories of Janey played on his mind: Janey sitting opposite him at Romano's before he flew off, declaring herself in her mini-mini-skirt transcendently ascending. Photographers had come: it was bliss: they had parted on the fashion page of next morning's paper.

"Six whole lines of blah-blah, Mark, what do you think? Gee, what a send-off."

At the airport, holding the folded paper gaily, George had looked around on the mob of little people there. And pitied them. Charitably, he hoped that some of them might be aware of his real presence in the foyer, and not just in print.

> Farewelling at Romano's yesterday, where George Molyneux dated Janey Rice for champagne and caviar. George has his sights on Harvard Business School and is, he says, remitting beauty for a while. Pity, but what a pity! We don't know what to wish Janey now, but some of you other guys might know. Anyhow, we're happy to publish all of her. Happy landing, George.

Great, just great, was what George said it was, boiling with zeal in the airport foyer, listening for the loudspeaker, thrilled to bits with those egregious hats that air-hostesses wear. Ten of them were standing in a row to take his ticket, which made them commonplace at once, but George didn't notice.

"I say," he said, "remitting beauty for a while? I never said that, and I wonder what it means. Remitting beauty?"

"Not to worry, George. The guy means that American women are lousy to look at. You're in for a pretty thin time."

"Oh, I don't think that. You're bulling me?"

No sense of humor, not good at his books, or even at games: everything about him tending to clog up in fatness: and yet Mark was, and had always been, perfectly aware that George would prosper. Even the Head at school had to go out of his way for George, because George would be standing there grinning and grinning and the Head would have to let off some witty profundity in acknowledgement, even if he had to shout it back along the cloisters. George knew how to show sincerity where it was due, and that was where it would do him a service some day.

George phoned his proposal to Janey. Standing on the sacred soil of Harvard he made it across the globe. Janey was at home in Pymble, roused out of bed and scratching her behind. Space love, that's what it was, boosted by the curve of the earth. Mark unkindly imagined George in his tie and tails, with a bunch of flowers in his hand, and Janey overlapping her pyjamas.

"Say that again, again please, George? It's terribly important." Some interstellar drift had got at George's voice. "Oh, now the line's so clear I can't believe it. Yes, I will, that's beaut, oh, George."

"Then meet me at Waikiki Beach. I'll book you from this end. We'll do it proud at Waikiki. Jet set for us, darling. Only famous places. Leave it all to me."

They must have done it at Waikiki. At some sumptuous hotel where you breathed air-conditioning. They saw the sea through acres of glass and from the roofs of mansions sensitive with concrete. And George put rings on her fingers and bells on her toes. They danced through the very latest in midnights, spontaneous with electric guitars and electric singers that unstrung the human voice and made it hot as metal. Then they came home and got married among their raw pinned-down acquaintances.

George had thereby declared himself and how his life would be. A phone-call to Perth or Los Angeles was how he liked to order his day. It kept him astride of the curve of the earth. His line was computers: main office, Sydney, branching out in Newcastle, if Newcastle meant to be with it. George and his firm meant to sell God Himself their brand of computers some day. But all evangelists are great with God and have his silent number.

And they all seem to come from America.

7

When she opened the door and saw three people standing there, Janey was under a strain at once. This was what it was like to be married? To be nice to all George's friends and their dogs, horses, or anything. Barefaced she was, barefooted, cleaning the house before lunch, virtuous and caught at it. Oh, she hadn't the time: why couldn't she just slam the door in their faces? But you couldn't do that.

Mark saw that Janey wasn't prepared to be nice till she'd had a shower at least. Also that her shirt was too intimate with her, too shrinky, did no more for her than half a window-curtain. There was Janey flopping about on the loose, dumpy as a pie on a plate.

"Oh, Janey, Janey, I see we should have phoned you first, I'm sorry. We've had an accident and I thought—"

"Oh, not at all, please do come in. We haven't got a phone yet, what a nuisance. How do you do? How are you? How'd you meet up with Mark? I hope—Not a bad accident, I hope? Yes, go straight in, forgive the mess. I was just cleaning up."

Mark was proud of Janey then, letting them see that he wasn't the complete hitch-hiker, but had friends in the world. He helped the ladies to their chairs.

"How's the baby going along?" he cheerfully asked.

"Baby!" Janey exclaimed, damned affronted, glancing at the other two women. Then she thought it best to pretend to be amused, and she half smiled. Women, just married, have to put up with far too much from silly ignorant young

26

men, and, there you are, it was what you got for having a callow kid for a best man. Talking nonsense to keep up with your experience.

"I'm feeling very well," Janey said, "if that's what you mean. There won't be any baby for months yet. Surely you can count, you students? We're only just—Oh, is there anything I can do for you two?"

Janey had just extricated herself in time. Only just married, she'd been going to say, and goodness knows what home truth that might have brought out, in the form of a joke. Mark was just a brash inexcusable young man, the commonest kind in Australia.

That afternoon Janey was going on about George's drip-dry shirts, when Mark suddenly grew conscious of this weeping in the kitchen, and the murmur of voices. He shot a look at Janey, but she persevered earnestly about the shirts, so she must have known what was going on long before he did. Mark got up and hopped about the floor. All he could see was Lin's dark-brown hair straggling over Biddy's shoulder and Biddy patting her back. He felt this anxious pang of envy. It didn't take women long to form a league. Bitterly, he returned to the purity of George's shirts.

"Of course, he needs a clean one every day," said Janey. "You men. And you still have to iron them, drip-dry or not."

"Mum complains, too," said Mark. "Gee, she's always complaining, but look here, Janey—? Janey, I'm sorry we've crashed in on you like this. My fault, all my fault, and I don't know what we should do yet."

"Oh, we could have some tea, couldn't we?" Janey said, a bit loudly, warning Lin and Biddy that she was coming.

That evening George, glad of the chance, kept on grousing genially.

"Well, frankly," he said, "I ask you. A fellah comes home

to this, poor bastard, when he's only five minutes married. But who's having a liqueur?"

With coffee and a good liqueur (in Newcastle, think of that), and the wife of his flesh, and a good day's business done, and three waifs to see how comfy he was, George was feeling good, real good. Young and well set up, with crystal stops to all his decanters, with his sideboard very broad and made of cedar from the early days, George had earned a merry thought as he poured out those liqueurs.

"Folks, I don't know how, but it reminds me, reminds me, somehow. Reminds me of that damn kitten he brought to our place once. You wouldn't believe it. Remember that, Mark? Said he'd managed to save one, and would I take it in? I mean, this kitten, for God's sake! Ha, ha, ha, oh, ha, ha, ha."

George was stopping up his decanter. He had the perfectly regular row of teeth that seems to go with no imagination.

"You see," said George, affably, "Mark and I were mates, though I'm a year or two older, I must admit. Do I have to say why?"

"No," said Lin, "don't bother. Besides, I know. It's because you were born a year or two sooner."

"Ha, ha, ha. Ha, ha, ha. Right, too," said George.

Then he cut the laughter and passed a liqueur to Biddy very efficiently, and to Lin with a cheeky challenge.

"Mark," he said, over his shoulder, "you can bloody well help yourself."

Mark was steering one to Janey's place while she was getting the coffee.

"You don't mind if I smoke, ladies?" said George, heartless with good manners again, for he was already taking out a cigar. With a cigar and a bow tie, George had noticed, you really had priority over everything else in your neighborhood: but Janey wouldn't let him wear a bow tie, for some reason. Ah, well, it didn't matter now. What he wanted to know, and had a right to know, was what the hell they were all doing, landing on him like this.

So they went over the accident again, and Lin had to pretend it was funny, for George's sake, and because it was evening, and them chatting.

"Relax, relax," George said. "Things happen, and it's lucky we were handy. Wasn't it, Janey?"

But Lin was thinking of her sister in Armidale, and this baby she'd just given birth to, and what would happen now? The guy was a student. They wouldn't be marrying, that's for sure. And that meant he would go away. Living together was okay, but guys like that don't encumber themselves. Maybe they wouldn't have the Volksy right tomorrow? All this easy chit-chat, she couldn't take it in. She had this itch to be off, even walking.

"Oh, no," Biddy was saying, "of course I wasn't going surfing. Having a few days off, that's all, before the summer prices go up. Can't afford a real holiday. And anyway, what's the use, by yourself?"

"More coffee, Biddy?" said Janey, quickly.

"No, thank you, dear," said Biddy.

And Mark was saying, "We'll just have to team up then, Biddy, won't we, and you'll have to come surfing after all?"

Biddy giggled at that, but she stroked her hair off her temple gingerly, too. Life was sadder than it looked, and she knew it. She was anxious for Lin, and how the conversation might turn on her, and what to say then.

"Where are you bound for, Lin?" said George. "Holiday, too, I suppose. All you lucky people."

George knew she was making for Armidale. Janey had told him, but he still wanted to hear it for himself and maybe learn something new and titillating.

"Mean to say," he said, "you're all a bit stranded, aren't you, well, just aren't you, thanks to me mate here? A man comes home and — Well, just aren't you?"

It was witty of George.

"I'm making for Armidale," said Lin. "To see my sister. Need to get there real soon, too. Real soon."

"Let's hope the car's okay tomorrow then."

"If not —"

"There's a train."

"I know but —"

"Your sister all right?" said Janey, sounding anxious.

"She's had a baby, a baby girl."

There was something too definite about Lin's tone. Ask all you like: go on, she was saying. But everybody knew that Biddy knew all about it, and it kept Biddy quiet. Soon they all went to bed, and Janey and George were very kind.

8

It was different with Mark, though.

Biddy and Lin slept in the in-laws' bedroom, on the twin beds. There was another bedroom with not a thing in it, and Mark offered to try it. If George took an end, they could move the couch from the living room and give him four walls of privacy around him.

"But what the hell?" George said. "You steering our furniture around?"

"Won't take a second," Mark said, softly, for you can't insist in another man's house, when you've brought him three awkward guests. And if you speak, you've got to choose, whether to speak softly or noisily. At least Mark spoke softly, in disputing.

George made a face, half bent over his end of the couch, but Janey was still pinning it to the floor with a real going-on of sheets and pillows. So George knew it was her house, if he wanted to live in it a happy man. And he straightened up again.

"There's no screen on the window," he said, decisively.

That finished it, and Mark slept in the living room. At least it's better than mosquitoes all night, to be caught sleeping beautifully by some spry woman in the morning. Mark was still a nervous boy, instinctively guarding himself. So he was awake when Biddy came in, and he'd expected Janey. The difference pleased him.

"Get up, Mark, please. Please to get up. Off with you to that garage as soon as it opens. I'll make you some tea first, but we have to get on."

She was in her dressing-gown, with tufts of well-slept upholstery appearing here and there, but Australia's an easy country.

"All right, all right, but what's the hurry, Bid?"

Mark was up on his elbow, not nervous now, but cheerful, yawning, scratching himself.

"I'll get up, okay. I want to get up," he said. "How'd you all sleep?"

On his way to the john, whistling ironically, he had this glimpse of George propped up on an extra pillow, whispering keenly into some gadget next to his neck. He had a letter in his other hand. But Mark resolutely pursued his drive to the john.

Funny, he thought, as he stood there.

So when he'd finished, he stood at George's door, politely screening himself from Janey, and barged in only with his voice,

"What's that, George, for God's sake?"

George went on with his whispering for another minute, snapped the thing shut, got up, laid it on the dressing table, and stood in the doorway in the full might of his pyjamas.

"It's a tape recorder, see?" he said, kindly. "And now I'm going to have a shower. Make yourself at home. In the living room," George called, stopping at the bathroom door, and thinking.

But Janey explained it, after, in the kitchen, over her cup of tea.

"You mean to tell me," Mark said, "he warbles business letters into that thing with you lying there?"

"And why not?" said Janey. "If he gets it done? Says it's a terrific start to the day."

"Yes, but—" Mark said.

It didn't fit with his idea that the summer was made for a wave and maybe for women as well. Marriage pillows couldn't be that serious so early, surely. It was tailoring things into the commuter's sham world. And here in his carelessness he'd dragged himself into a bit of boring business, too. He'd better be off to that garage.

And the garage man showed him the contempt he deserved. Often, they don't even look at you, garage men: standing there rubbing the muck off their hands, gazing at grease and flanges. This mechanic's name was Cyril, which is one hell of a name for a mechanic. A hand-rolled cigarette was poking out of his mouth, and he had great lines on his cheeks, incised like wheelrims, for men grow to be like their trade. He wore nothing but his own body-hair and a jumpsuit, open from neck to navel. Mark could see the top of a jockstrap, but a roll of flesh was threatening it, and creeping on slowly. His hair was black as a field of beans, and boastful.

A voice interrupted, crying through the shed.

"This Vauxhall job's down for today, Cyril. I'll put Max on it, right now. It's a bit of a bastard."

But they rarely swear, these men, in the course of their jobs, for they have patience with the terribleness of metal, and nuts, and bolts. Crude words are more liable to issue from drawing-rooms now, and journalists, and relaxing joyous professors. The swing to the left, that's what it is. Cyril might have been reflecting on this as he drew on his cigarette. His eye was suffering a lot.

"You was saying?" observed Cyril.

"Would the — I've come about the Volksy and the A40."

"Oh, that." There was a gleam in Cyril's sad eye again. "Yes, mate. A minute, will yah? Put Max on it. T'fix th'exhaust. I'll 'ave a look at the bleed'n Volksy. Could be a write-off, mate. A proper write-off. Fool thing to do, who-ever done it."

"Yes," said Mark. "It was only a slight touch, not much, really, but it doesn't take much."

"Could 'ave screwed the whole damn engine, though. That's what. Clean off its seating."

"Can it be fixed today?"

"No, nor any day that I can see coming. Any insurance on it?"

"Don't know."

Cyril was inured to the hopeless ignorance of customers, and made his living by it. Stoically, he drew on his cigarette, scrutinized it, pinged it as far as he could out into the street.

"It's not my car," Mark said, before he embittered himself completely.

"Ugh," said Cyril. "What you on about then? Bullocksing my time away."

"It's Lin's," Mark said. "Bird I ran into."

"Tole you then," said Cyril, wearily, rolling another ciga-rette. "Not today, nor tomorrow, nor maybe not the next day, either. Max, you got that exhaust fixed up yet? Comin' to do the rest. A40's okay," Cyril said, raking through his tools. "All the oil drained off? It's a cow this bloody back-axle, never seen such a cow."

Standing around, hoping, you get tons of information if you want it.

Lin met Mark on his way back, for she couldn't rest. Coming toward him in the morning and making nothing of it, she cheered him up. They stopped, and he told her about Cyril.

"Anyway," he said, "I'm sorry, Lin, and I'm gonna pay you it all back, even if it means working for the rest of my life."

"Gee, you're a funny boy."

"Well, thanks, it's a compliment."

"How is it?"

"You can't call me funny without having thought it out."

"If a boy — Gee, if any boy rams you in the tail some time, you can't help but notice, can you? It's practically rape."

They laughed, but then Mark was rueful.

"Well, if it was, I didn't notice. I'm sorry about that, too."

"But let's stop this, shall we? I don't need jokes to be sick on, not just at present. Or at any time. Do you?"

She even sounded interested in whether he did or not. Mark stole her hand for a moment, but she stole it away.

"Do you?" she persisted.

"I take it back," he said, "but only so far. I couldn't have hurt you like that. Nor anyone else," he said.

He put his arm about her flimsy middle for any curious housewife to see, and held on, and made her walk back. She didn't fend him off, but suddenly confided in him, and the horny looks of the truck drivers were all wasted, or wasted on each other, in the early sun.

34

"It's not a nasty matter," Lin said.

"No, it isn't. Say, why couldn't the three of us just set out for Armidale in the A40? Today?"

"Should have gone to this garage myself," she said, instead of answering. "You come and tell me my car's a write-off and then you say, Come in ours, and—"

"Well, and we could pick up yours."

"And you haven't got a car," Lin said.

"But Biddy has, and you've been talking, and she must have suggested it, even. It'd sweeten the world a bit, if we all did that."

He was asking her about much more than the car, for she was the woman and he was still a boy, standing on top of a great mountain range and looking west into a far country, rolling with promises. It makes you look, and look again, and feel pleased with all your breath. Auburn Lin's hair was, a shade that slipped in between his discriminations, but shiny in the sun. As they came nearer Janey's house, they walked much more distinctly like two people.

"What's wrong with your sister, Lin? Why don't you tell me?"

Lin stopped, and looked him over coolly, as though they really were old friends and he could stand the scrutiny.

"You mightn't like it, that's why. And it's not your business yet, is it? It's more important than any car engine, or wave. You'll see. If you're not to be a fool all your days. Boys, they're all right when everything's pleasant. And when it's not, you turn to women, see if you don't. Cheer up, it's not your affair, and I wouldn't buy into it, if I were you. Carry on with your dream."

Almost bitter she was, going on. If he hadn't liked her so much, he'd have said she *was* bitter, and blaming him. She assumed that he would duck and sheer away, as though he were only a gull or a tern or a shag on the shore. It spoiled his breakfast for him. Bitterness warps all prettiness away.

She seemed to have it in for men. If that was what the new equality did, it wasn't much to anybody's advantage. Oh, well, maybe it was the loss of the Volksy, and the irritation of delay, and wondering who would pay up in the end, and all those practical matters. She looked good-natured, not hard.

9

Watching Lin as she got up from table and took her watch off and started managing the sink, Mark could see that she was mighty pleasant in everybody's eyes. He ferried back and forth his offerings of dirty plates and spoons, and she paid no heed, as though he had been always there. The conversation, to a man looking for a wave, was abysmal. He made a nuisance of himself with marmalade, and where to put the butter, and where the slops went and the scraps, but they went at it relentless. He found himself noticing how Lin's hair was much fairer on her forearm and the knowledge entered into his possessions. George went off to work and Biddy was settled with cigarette and paper, and suddenly the world was good.

"Oh, I usually buy my coffee medium ground, Mocha and Kenya."

"I prefer American blend, I think, but I like a change, too."

"Mind you, George likes to grind it himself. Hoards the smell of it."

"Oh, does he?"

"He's funny. They're so carnal, men."

"Is that what? Yes, put it down, that's where it goes, can't you see? I like this hot-plate of yours, Janey."

"Oh, another present. But I was so vexed; the heat came through the bottom. Spoiled all the top of the gate-leg table. It's why we keep a runner on. Mahogany's so easy to mark. It's quite an heirloom or we wouldn't have it. First time I saw George furious."

"No wonder, either. Is this the detergent you use?"

"Yes, only a little. You find it hard on the hands? I've gloves if you want."

"I'll use this mop. Won't put my hands in much. It's my nails that get ruined. No, I'll wash and you can dry. Don't hustle me."

So he dried up and it was better, because he could look at her all the time, with her hair getting in her eyes and her hands wet.

"Try this fork, why don't you."

But she wouldn't. Went on talking to Janey, as though his suggestions were a daily cause of patience between them. He saw Janey look and smile, and Biddy wasn't reading her paper, much.

"No news is there, Biddy, this morning?"

Strange how the summer was becoming much more serious than he had meant, and yet he was enjoying it more. Girls grew up and dragged you after. Here he was drying dishes, and not only that, but keen on it.

"Funny," he said to Biddy, in the shelter of the other voices, "girls pretend the kitchen's no place for them, but they're kidding themselves, surely?"

But the whole interest in hot-plates and coffee blends collapsed at once.

"Yeah, yeah?"

"You wanna get wise to yourself."

"Have this whole bloody sink."

It doesn't matter who said what.

"I was only talking to Biddy now," said Mark.

"What do you think?" said Biddy. "Every young man's their business. They'll hear every word you say, you should know that already."

"But oh, what crap."

"Yes, bullshit, Biddy, just. Who's side are you on, anyway?"

Biddy laughed, because she liked laughing. Sometimes the main need seems to be to have the same liberated words as men. And it encouraged Mark.

"I only meant, if you think home's a good thing, how it needs a woman, maybe. It's no home by yourself. It just descends to farting. Which isn't funny, all by yourself. Needs—"

But they didn't like that, and wanted it done with, and Mark stopped.

"You're not as LIB as you say?"

"Oh, dear, no we're not," said Lin.

And he was relieved that she answered then. "You see," he said, "it's so silly. There's men that never will let you win at words like that. We're too adolescent, I suppose."

"Let's—"

"—not debate it."

"I wouldn't call it a home without a man, a decent man," said Janey. "He's equally necessary to me."

"I'm sorry for what I said just now," said Mark.

Men have to be kept in check by silence itself, but something else had to be said then.

"If you just mean," said Lin, desperately, "that the woman has to stay home and dust and wash up and sing to herself—"

38

"And keep the cupboards stocked up and the meals ready—"

"And sex it up with her husband whenever *he* says—"

"And fuss about him when his throat's sore—"

"And be put off with a bunch of flowers now and then—"

"And a trip to the dump with the rubbish—"

"She's got a life of her own to live, and nobody's asking you."

"Funny," Mark said, "we were all so happy, lately."

"You asked for it," said Biddy, "and you know it, too. These girls are different, different from my time, but they're not tartars. They're so much the same that it's always sad. Cleaning up as they deny it. And him helping."

"Liking it, too, up till lately."

"And the women like me," said Biddy, "we see it all, and we size it up, and the thing we say is, She'll make him a good wife, or He'll make a good husband to her. The old standards all the time. And that's what they want, if they could have it."

"Yes, but—," said Lin, turning back to the sink. "But girls, the world's opener for them. They'd be hermits in hell if they refused."

"Refused what?" said Mark.

"I suppose so," Biddy said, and sounded tired. "Still, it's like eating all the sweets in the shop. That way none of them's good."

"I know that, too," said Lin.

Mark didn't know anything about Biddy then, or Lin either. At the back of Biddy's life was her dead husband that she'd nursed through three or four years of painful illness and made herself sleepless in the process. It was no wonder she got up first that morning. And Lin? There was her sister in the hospital, and what's more, standing like the ghosts of Banquo's children? Lin wasn't really as embattled as

Janey was. Her swear words jarred. Lin wasn't sure of a house and every happiness. All she was sure of was that she would like it. But these sorrowful matters weren't allowed to appear.

There's a deep proportion, and it's not equality. Far better that each should be superior here and there, and show some trust.

Biddy went away to tidy her bedroom, Janey was busy in the kitchen, in the living room Mark sorted out his gear. Lin went to the garage by herself, and soon came back saying that the A40 was ready and that they'd try and have the Volksy moving by tomorrow.

"Sorry, Janey," Lin said, "but I asked them about a place and they said I might get a bed at the Carlton. So I'll go over there now."

"Oh, Lin, but I'd be so hurt. What's another night, with the beds slept in already. And George, well, it gives him a change from his wife, doesn't it?"

George might have been whingeing just a tiny bit.

"Oh, well," said Mark, "supposing I slept in the shed? I've got to save up till tomorrow, so I can't afford the Carlton."

"He was our best man," Janey said. "I don't know why."

"Say, girls, let's go to the beach, shall we, and stop this moping?"

This second suggestion of his seemed to lift the weight of the day, and they got ready. Lin was still looking out of hooded eyes, picking things up and laying them down again. Mark hoped the sun might shine it away. There was a picnic to get, and the A40 to fetch, and twenty-three dollars to pay for it, too. When you step into the world, he thought, you sure do have to keep your money handy.

But as they were driving away, Janey said,

"I wonder, Mark, would you kindly stop at a phone-box, please?"

40

It was a premeditated, quiet question, and they stopped at a phone-box quietly. Little mystifications and necessities, that's what women were made of, Mark thought, not sugar and spice. It made him yearn for a breath of men's company, even if they wanted to scrounge five dollars off him, which would be cheaper, after all. While Janey was out, Lin and Biddy in the back seat just mourned out at their separate windows, and he let them.

Janey came back, sat down breezily, and they drove off. For a bit she didn't even direct him, but then she eased his way as though she had suddenly forgotten she was married. He put his left arm over the wheel and peered earnestly through the windshield. He was better pleased with Janey, of course, but not all that much.

"Mark, I was talking to George, on the phone. You're not angry?"

"No," he said. "I can stand anything. Be gentle with me."

Janey slid away a bit, but she came back again.

"Mark, they—can't you see, Mark? They're not all that keen on the beach."

"Oh, that? I must confess you've hit it."

"Mark, there's a beaut yacht we could take. I asked George. It's his father's yacht. They're coming up for January. Living on it."

"On the sea?"

"No, not the sea. On Lake Macquarie."

"Hell, Janey, but what's the matter with me? Girls, they've always got to be thinking of something better, now haven't they? Just like Mum."

It made a stir at last in the back seat. He swore gently at the ugly street, fixed Lin in the mirror, but couldn't get her face to budge.

"It does get you, though. And then they tell you you're petted, for goodness' sake. Just a petted boy, that's what they say."

Janey was silent, so she was probably thinking it, too. And Lin there like a load of nothing, and Biddy anxious, eye on the traffic.

"Anyway, think about it," Janey said at last. "Yacht's at Belmont, five minutes away. I'll show you, just in case."

"Just in case what?"

"In case you like the idea," Janey said, with grieving charm. And she turned and spoke to the others about some cookie shop they were passing. Immediately, as usual, he began to feel stupid and ashamed.

"All right, Janey, all right, I was wrong. Let's go to Belmont. Have a good day. You tell them. See what they think. Gee, I'm sorry, I'm sorry."

All sitting there, he thought, indulging his selfishness, pretending the only thing they wanted to see was a wave. What could Biddy do with it, think of that? But you saw older women swimming, and appearing to like it. Maybe he just didn't understand women, not at all. And that apology was still far too peremptory, to cover his anguish up. But they would understand his clumsiness, he hoped: and think him uncertain, not vain.

"Maybe they won't like it any better," Janey said, soothingly. "But, I think, *you* might. It's fun."

There was far more to Janey than he'd guessed, and he acknowledged it. Out loud, men have the say, but only if they never grow up, maybe. You begin to co-operate, if you're any good at all. If you don't, it can't be said that you like the birds, but only yourself. Mark could see it already.

They were glad of any difference, Biddy and Lin, for the sake of novelty. Water, and three sad girls, and summer sunshine. All they needed besides was tons of burn cream for a perfectly beaut day. And floppy hats: did they have floppy hats?

"Yes, I put them in. Thinking of the beach, of course. Wasn't it lucky?" Janey smiled. "They're in the trunk."

Mark was laughing at himself.

"Thanks, Janey, and good for you. You can have two Electric Portable Hand Mixers."

10

Maybe it was the splendid view ahead that lured her. Anyhow, very gradually, as they sailed the reaches of Lake Macquarie, Lin edged her way up the racing deck and lay in the bow. But then there was all this tossing about: she seemed not to know whether she wanted to lie on her back or on her belly. Sometimes she lay with her chin in her hands and spied beyond the line of hills to the west. Sometimes a house on a westward point would be sitting ideal among grass and trees, with the slope of paradise, which is fifteen degrees down to the water, with a little jetty of its own and a spit of sand to sit on, and the fresh light of morning saying: Behold, I make all things new. Kind of biblical it was, and early, a shining world, but with more water than the Bible has, mostly. And sometimes she would lie on her back and watch the leach and luff of the sail traveling up to the top of the mast and clean into the still, blue sky.

Mark caught Biddy's eye and had to confess that he'd been watching Lin.

"Isn't she a moody one?" he said.

Biddy shook her head. "Go on. Go up and speak to her."

Old-fashioned match-maker, they're still about. She was a kind, unselfish person Biddy, and she couldn't be young herself. But she was acquainted with death, and she thought the remedy for death was love, to keep the world green. Besides, she liked these two.

And Mark had been passing solitary men baling out in boats, men that bent a quizzical eye and saw that Janey was the sailor. He was quite ready to go for'ard when Biddy said.

But Lin was so far away that she started, sat up, shook herself like a dog, glanced suspiciously at the other two women.

"You think I'm worrying about my sister? You think I'm worrying about my car? Don't you?"

"Oh, I'm not thinking about you. Much. It's a lie: what's bothering you, Lin?"

"Isn't this a lovely place? You drive up and down on the road, and you never see Lake Macquarie."

So she wasn't telling him.

"Yes, it was a great idea of Janey's. Must admit."

"What are you going to be, Mark?"

"A teacher. I haven't thought about it, why? I think I'd like to be a teacher because it's a young job."

She seemed almost to envy him, and it's not everybody that envies a teacher. You might even have to be careful how you confess to it.

"I was going to be a journalist," she said. "D'you think—? Oh, what's the use?"

"Do I think what?" Mark already knew that she was a cadet journalist.

"Do you think any job's worth it? You bump into somebody, say you're sorry, and then you're off again."

"What's the connection?" Mark said. "That's not what we're doing, is it?"

She looked at him, and nodded, and kept on, and stared at him.

"That's it," she said, picking something final off her knee.

44

She keeled over and lay flat out with her fists kneading her cheeks and her face comical as a gnome's. "Life's just a rude mess, isn't it?"

Gunwale to gunwale, they agreed about that.

"But you've made friends of Biddy and Janey?"

"Oh, they've been so kind: of course. I've just got to get away. Can't lie about here, pretending. Pretending we're nymphs and shepherds. All you're looking for is a wave, anyway."

"Don't care if I never find it. Here with a loaf of bread beneath the bow. You know those cyclones they seek out, don't you? Call them by pet names like Althea, or Amaryllis, or Mavis? Well, I've found my wave and it's called Lin."

You smile sadly then, and she did.

"Big thrill for you. All the summer to look for a wave, it cuts us back to nothing, right enough. And yet I like you," she said, "you're not all silly, not really reckless. Student stirrers, they're so upstart. And you're not one, after all. Thanks for bumping into me: you're a damn nuisance, but thanks."

She wriggled and nudged his shoulder gently, but quite enough to make him collapse and grab her. Tenderness, if you're too young for it, is rough at first.

"Take care, take care," he said, from among her hair, "or we might be happy."

"Hey, you Mark, we're going about now. What you up to? Stand by to tack the sail."

Janey was noisier than usual, and gratified.

"You can go for'ard again after," she said. "Isn't it a nice sail we're having?"

Mark had seized the rope—or sheet, was it?—cursing those absurd words that sailors use.

"Yes," he said. "Aye, aye, sir. Look here, can I hitch this sail over now?"

"Just wait till I tell you, will you, or we'll all drown."

At the appointed time, Mark fixed the rope and scrammed.

"There was my boss, you know," Lin said. "Young, TV sort of chap. Twenty-eight or so, old enough to be married once or twice. You know his idea of his job? It was just to get me to bed. You know that?"

"And—Did he?" Mark said.

"I'm twenty-one," said Lin, as if that were an answer. "Much older than you," she said, rolling away.

They lay on their elbows for pillows, looked at each other, had this sensation of drinking.

"Funny, but we're nothing to each other. Isn't it funny?"

Mark didn't think it funny.

"Mean to say," said Lin, "frittering their days away, chasing scandal. Where's the use of reading it, even on the train?"

"Oh, I see. We're back at the job again."

He wasn't disappointed. He liked to hear her unveil herself, swish the curtains back. You had to get to know your girl friends.

"I got this compassionate leave to see my sister. Cadets don't usually get it with Christmas coming on. Don't know if I'll go back. Didn't mean to. Meant to write and tell them my sister was too bad . . . Anyway, I belong among the small towns. And they can't stay dead. There must be more than Sydney."

"Armidale? But it's a city, too. Calls itself a city?"

"Why should it be so eager? Look at this."

She turned to the sun on Lake Macquarie.

11

"Biddy?" Mark said, catching her alone for a minute when they were back and were parking the A40 to be out of George's way.

"Yes, love, what?"

"Why does Lin look on me as just another whistle-stop station?"

"Maybe because you're a hitch-hiker. People don't credit them much, do they? They're frail, and pass away."

"Well, that's true, I suppose."

"Besides, there's two things on her mind. And she thinks they'll multiply. She's wise enough."

"If one's the car—"

"Oh, no, not the car, that's only one of the multiplications. There's her young sister—"

"And she's had a baby."

"—that she's always had to look after, it seems. And she's had a baby, yes."

"Well, it can't affect—"

"And the second thing is her sister's boy friend. Lin says he's taken off. Left her, baby and all. And she's not out of hospital."

"I suppose," said Mark, "she could have expected—? I suppose it happens. Suppose he thinks the baby's—not in the bargain—a kind of a give-away—for adoption, maybe?"

He was going on, trying to be pleasant, to put in the man's view, and he hadn't met this sister. At the university, girls dropped out now and then, and sometimes they came back after, looking just as beautiful, and their lives composed. You couldn't see behind their knowledgeable eyes. But Biddy was, on the sudden, furiously angry.

"Shut up," she said, "if that's all you have to say." And then she thought of something else. "Trouble is, Lin says he meant to stay by her and the baby. Oh, well. Can't tell," said Biddy. "Suppose he's just scrammed, that's all. But she says there's more to it."

Mark was careful to say nothing else. Hadn't he set out, only two days ago, to have a glorious time as long as summer lasted? You were on the move, and that way all you needed was the surface of life, nipping away from its problems and into the good time. Nothing would ever catch up.

"She can't get rid of this hunch," Biddy said.

Later, too, he heard what George had to say, out in the garage, when the evening was breaking up and men have to come out with home-truths or leave them unsaid for ever. "You've two alternatives," George said crisply, expelling smoke through his teeth till he had achieved a really awesome pause. And then he just said it again. "You've two alternatives. You either thumb it up the coast at first light tomorrow, or make love to the lass all day."

"Why so?"

"Come off it. Isn't it bloody obvious? You're not going to pay this bill, are you?"

"That's just what I was thinking."

"Look here you old sod, you don't live in the world, do you? If you think the insurance will come and pay you back, when you've already shelled out—"

"But I don't think so. To hell with insurance."

"Goat," said George. "What's insurance for, but to pay for crumpled tin?"

George took a pace out into the night and was amazed at the innocence of the rest of the world.

"Maybe so," Mark said. "But I was driving and I know I

was wrong, and at the time I said I'd pay. There were two women there. Oh, maybe I was acting Sir Galahad and it's not much done, but I'm sticking to it. I know you would have managed it better. Anyway, how would loving her help?"

"Go on? You must see that. Could even love her myself, no trouble."

"You stick to your own toaster," Mark said.

"Look, you bastard, if you were to love her in the friendliest way, she couldn't keep you to it, could she?"

"Keep me to what, for the Lord's sake?"

"You old bastard," said George again, "you know what I mean. There's no debts between friends. You can't have sex AND bills, not with a decent bird. Depend on it, she'll wipe the whole lot."

George knew about these matters, you could see. Obligation just faded into the distance, You forgot, and the girl stayed too friendly to remind you. In time she forgot, too.

"Wipe the whole lot," George repeated, with telling eloquence. "You've got to look at it like this. Now they come armed for the battle: it's only a game. You tilt a lance and they take it there. And off you both go looking for another. Just boomps-a-daisy, that's all. Or else you look for a wave," George said, laughing, "if it's outdoor sport you fancy."

He was perfectly brilliant about it.

"Is that it, Big Chief?"

"That's it, boy," said George hoarsely, like a movie lover. "They can take it just the same as men. In fact, they all want it. No moping for nine months, no feeling you've done them in. You've tickled them nicely, that's all. Ships that pass in the night, get it?"

"Got it," Mark said. "Think I'll try your first alternative, thanks. Think I'll try my thumb."

"That'll be hilarious," George said, "but, man, hilarious. Let me know how it goes."

And he screamed with laughter: but, gee, was he witty!

"Night, night, married man. Night, night, Georgy boy," yelled Mark.

George, it was plain, couldn't get by on love alone. He needed lust as well, and he maybe even supposed that everybody needed it. And what if he was right, too, in these dry days? Mark went in and rolled on his pillow. He'd been to Cyril's place and he knew the Volksy was there to pick up in the morning. He knew the price of it, too, he'd been to the Post Office, and he had the money on him, standing there chortling with George. It could have taken him to Darwin, all the way, given good truckers.

Mark tossed on his pillow. Debts seemed to be something for any proud man to incur, a part of the sheer bitterness of growing up. He'd seen them do it to him. And maybe George was right about Lin, too. What did Mark know about it? She hadn't told him how she responded, that time, when her boss came sniffing.

You can torment yourself on your pillow, spoil all your attitudes, boil your brain into a smoking dump, and taint everybody with it. It was long after midnight before he fell asleep, but by that time he had begun to think of Lin's auburn hair spilling on another pillow.

In the morning, as soon as the place was open, he paid and got free of Cyril and his mob, and brought back the Volksy. Nobody knew anything until it was there at the gate. Then, standing at the gate in the perpetual sun, they all saw Lin off.

"I'd better be getting along then, hadn't I? Out of your way. Thanks ever so much, Janey. Thanks, all of you. Shan't—I shan't forget. I'll need you to think about."

But what do you say? Biddy was crooning and waving at

every little speech, with Lin there, framed in the window, fingering her beads, struggling with the rough morning sun.

"Well? Here it is. Got to fight my way into Thursday. May I look in on the way back, please, Janey? I'd like to. Thank you for being so kind to me. Don't like saying goodbye."

Come on, George, what do you say now? Mark was kicking himself plenty, and wishing everybody else gone, resenting them all. For it was his doing that they were friends.

"Goodbye, Biddy," she said, last of all, and smiled with her eyes, and drew away.

Just that glimpse of a girl's fine mouth, and then only the blank back of her head, devoted to such a silly thing as driving. She *wasn't* as hardboiled as George would have made her. And yet $136.20 was a lot of money to throw away on any wench, however she might ring true, if you weren't going to see her again. And it's such an empty business, to be just nothing to somebody you like.

George, at any rate, was feeling a credit to himself. He turned as the car was receding, and found his voice,

"Course, there's still a hell of a lot to be done to that Volksy. Hope she gets there, that's all. Must've done the body work with their bare fists."

"Of course," Mark was saying, as he went on. "But there wasn't any time for body work."

"And when are you pushing off, old boy?"

"Hell, but I nearly —"

"Oh, Janey, Janey," Biddy chipped in, much flustered. "Oh, Janey, you've been so very nice, and patient. I was thinking — just to see everything tidy, and be off. Shan't take long."

"I nearly went off in the Volksy," Mark was saying. "But I wasn't asked."

Janey was a bit mad at George, but she might have said

something, in their private sheets, that encouraged his downrightness. And he had to invent himself a sense of humor, too.

12

"Well," Biddy said, "which is it to be? The country or the coast?"

"The coast," said Mark. "I'm looking for a wave. Didn't you know?"

They were sitting by Hexham Bridge over the Hunter River where Biddy had drawn into the curb. You can't allow your whole life to be altered just because you bump into a girl's tail, can you? In two days if he persevered, the past would go out like the tide and life would be its ordinary self again. Nevertheless, he was relying just a little bit on Biddy's preference for the Hunter Valley, inland.

And yet you know how this country looks in summertime? Hot and greedy as a grasshopper. All those acres of wilting fields with coal underneath them, and the bits of scruffy bush with every tree too tired to hold its leaves up, and the birds lumbering about like flying clodhoppers in the sick air. And then if you've ever been near Hexham Bridge, you'll know it's a pile of railway lines and warehouses that are just shacks of corrugated iron with God's light on them, and they make the very view ill-natured. And there's the blazed road, and all the wires and poles, the river crawling away into the mangroves, the Catholic cemetery despairing among the long grass, a strip of housing by the highway, and miles and miles of flat land wearing away into the west. At Hexham Bridge, surely, anybody would reach for the sea.

Well, maybe not Biddy. She'd been driving, and still was.

"There'll be plenty of time for a wave," she said. "They'll keep coming in. Couldn't—"

"I don't think I could, really," Mark said. "And on the beach—On the beach you don't get poor so quickly."

And he gave a sigh that broke into a smile, but it still made Biddy trembly about the mouth. Some old folks feel, where money is concerned, that they should never let a young person cough up, no matter what he has done. It amused Mark, and touched him, too, so that his smile grew kinder.

"It's okay, Biddy," he said. "We're square, aren't we?"

"I'll pay a bit of that back, by Monday. It was my fault, too, for keeping you talking."

"No, it wasn't. And I can't string along till Monday, sorry. I mean, okay at Janey's house where it was civilized, but, say we were to go up the coast, we take different sizes in waves, don't we?"

He was half trying to kid her into coming, yet.

"Mark," Biddy said, refusing to joke, "I *was* going up the coast, but not now. I'm only taking a day or two off, you know. I've two boarders, and they're away for the moment. It's a humdrum deadening thing to do, to look after two strong men that just let you go on looking after them. You wouldn't need to care about them," Biddy said, "for they never give you a thought. Still, I've got to do it."

"Cheer up then, Bid, you're twice as well off. You've only one strong man beside you now, and he likes you a lot."

"Mark," said Biddy, "I've made up my mind. I'm going up the valley. I promised Lin. And I thought then, you might—"

"No, Biddy, no. You shouldn't have been counting on me, then. It's all right for you, but why should I fall for it? It would be silly. I'm off up the coast."

When you are treading on the edge of a very brief acquaintance, and one that somehow has seemed more than that, there's this acute uneasiness, and it's hard to suppress. You draw up your arms, stretch your legs, smile as comfortably as you can, snarl out a yawn, but it won't go.

"Then you'd better get out here? Hadn't you? Sorry I can't take you further. You'll have to go by the bridge?"

"All right, if that's what you want."

She looked at him and nodded, and they were both uncertain. She was already being wounded by the next few minutes.

"Best thing we could do," he said, sitting still.

But, if that was so, then why not do it? With one action he heaved his gear from the back seat with one arm and opened the door with the other. He was out, standing up, and his knees were saying goodbye to Biddy. He couldn't find the proper shoulder for his gear.

"So long," he said, to the sliding roof.

"Sure you won't come, Mark? It would only —"

"No," he said, "so long."

You have to bang those old A40 doors, and it sounds so rough. He walked back a few yards to give her a start, saw her look in the mirror, for him first, then for the traffic. When she went off at last, she gave it far too much throttle. She waved, hooted, changed gear, veered away over the railway. She didn't change into high till she was far around the bend. Funny old Biddy.

And when this happens, if you're a young fellow taking a vacation on the cheap, as you've a perfect right to, you stand fast on the roadway, lift your wind-jammer by the collar high above your head, slam it back on your shoulder, and

start to use your thumb. You might have vindicated yourself. You can't be spending all your life with women.

Emma Beach is a very little beach south of Foster, and he
had his eye on that. You come upon it through the Myall
Lakes, turning off the highway under Beulahdelah Mountain which, for the last twenty miles before the turn-off, has
been giving you back your passion for the landscape. You
twist with the road and bob up and down, but there it is in
front for a reminder of nobility. If you had eyes and could
see only hills, even the dry hills of this continent, you could
have enough of history to steady you. For wind and sun
through the lapse of time have brought them everything.

And below them, and well off the highway, are the Myall
Lakes: peaceable water skirted by petticoats of trees, and
through the leaves and black branches the water shines far
darker blue, and there's boats tied up in lonely places, and
grebe and moorhen and heron on holiday, and the blue sky
bends over all. You can feel content with the tiny touch of
man's hand in a countryside of nameless events. Not even
the seasons show very much difference at noonday. But life
passes across, and what it passes across is beautiful.

Mark knew the district and he asked the trucker he was
with to let him off at a little wooden bridge with some cot-
tages beyond it, so that he could walk past for the freedom
of it and enjoy on his own legs a few miles of summer's day.
His driver, cowering into the door of his truck, looked over
at him with misgivings.

"All right," he said, hauling on the hand-brake. "If that's
how you want it, ta-ta."

Now that the roads are made for engines, it's almost eerie
to find anyone who volunteers to walk on them, and the
walker himself, as the cars go by, feels outcast and unex-

plained. Besides, with no trucker to speak to, his mind kept lapsing into the last few days in all their unsatisfactoriness. He took with him to Emma Beach a tinge of disappointment. The nor'-easter was too sudden and too cool after the closeness of the road through the bush. He sat on the sand in late afternoon when the cold blue was already domineering the eastern sky. The lump of a cargo boat was edging far out, making the emptiness clumsy. He didn't feel the slightest urge to take a wave, but he made himself do it, after coming so far and so obstinately. And it gave him an exuse to have a shower. You feel self-conscious by yourself, and he thought he could hardly march out hot from the bush and take a shower just like that, when the showers had been put there to get you clear of salt, and nothing else. And anyway the showers were in the camping area, which wasn't for those that came on foot. There was no scale of payment for just flesh and blood. So he hired a blanket and slept on the beach. He had to say he was from No. 7, a great plush house trailer that he rather fancied. With his day behind him and a wave taken, with his shower and his single blanket, and the whole of the summer ahead, it was as comfy all night as he could imagine. The only trouble was that he had two hip-bones with no imagination at all.

And in the morning, when it was utterly beautiful, as it always is when the veils come off in the dawn, he still couldn't get in tune. Everything was just as deserted as the night before.

You climb a steep hill for your breakfast at Emma Beach, if you have to buy it at the store, and you tend to bolt it among the crowd that forms around the door and counter. There seems no hope to be had in sitting down, except that it seems to put you more in the company of the flies. But you come up the steep hill again for your lunch, because you can't take it with you and bury it in the sand all morning, and even without sand the thought of cold pork pie and peas would bruise your gut like a stone. So, with magnificent goodwill to everything, Mark lay and stared at the ocean. At least he was getting brown. Anyway, often enough, even with the family, it could be boring, really boring, on holiday. But one thing was sure, he wouldn't ever in his life come by himself again. There were all sorts about, especially mums and kids, but he left them enjoying themselves between the surfing flags, or building sand-castles. As a sheer spectator, you can soon disapprove of the human race if you aren't careful.

Biddy would be up at Armidale by now, and they could have been eating decent meals all the way and conducting life as if it weren't quite so lonely, and with something real to do. You underrate people when you're with them, but why did he need to insist on being bored like this? It wasn't that he was missing Lin, oh no. There were plenty of birds going by, each one brown as a cup of tea, wasp waist shrinking lusciously into navel, all the middle of her full of sea-air and rejoicing, and as soon as he felt like it he could make up to one, and she'd be pleased, of course. He knew it was savage to assume that, but in your imagination you take revenge on others for your own shortcomings. In the afternoon, though, a bloke came over instead.

Mark had been surfing, but it's so terribly businesslike with waves to rush in on and fight out of and rush in on again, and it contradicts the straggliness of waves if you're too disciplined about them. So he was back on the beach on one elbow stroking his tan when this bloke came over. A bloke that wore a black wind-breaker totally out of place. Mark took to him at once, with his gauntlets and goggles to match, and greased black hair. Even if he was going to do the Nazi goose step, he was welcome.

"How yah, mate, how yah get to that beach over there? Buggers me, but you tell me, go on."

Kept sending these little telegrams, as though he were accustomed to work in the Post Office. And of course he was only being polite to swear at you first, and put you at your ease.

"Lazarus Beach, you mean? That's easy as crap. You can't have looked?"

"Well, maybe not proper. Not long enough to find it, anyway."

"Not proper, for sure, kiddo."

Mark was going out of his way in his language, too. You did that, when you admired a new bloke.

"Orright," he said, "orright. Keeps on ending up at some factory, road does. Bloody great headland. No chance of getting at what you see there."

And he pointed with his hand.

"Fisherman's Beach you've been at. Can't see anything for spray. No, that's not it."

"This Lazars Beach then?" he said, not interested.

"Lazarus Beach. You got your bike handy?"

"Yip," he said. He capitulated nicely. "Up there at the park."

"Come on then, I'll show you. Wouldn't mind a ride on a bike, either, just at this moment. Everything's so damned beautiful I'm nearly dead. With envy," Mark said.

It puzzled this bloke, though. He made to say something else quick, so that his puzzlement wouldn't show.

"Chain Gang's on the way, see. Gotta spot a place, a likely place for them. Has to be private, Bus says, real private."

"What's the chain gang?"

"Chain Gang? Name of our mob. Bikies. We're the Chain Gang."

"Sounds—kind of grisly. D'you mean it?"

"Bus means it, he means it orright. Not bike chains, yah know. Chain gang, convicts, road-makers, blazing the trail, all that. Get it?"

58

"Who's Bus?"

"The big chief. Smart guy, Bus."

"Must be, if he's got a sense of history on a motor-bike!"

"Sure does," he said, but only because Mark was asking a question. He didn't have much sense of history himself, not to give him any judgment. It's not a local thing. You'd think the winds have only blown off and on this coast since statistics were kept.

"What's your name?"

"They call me Par. What's yours?"

"Mine's Mark."

"Pleased to meet you, Mark."

And then, so help me, if they didn't have to stop and shake hands, which Mark hated. Scraping up the dregs of good manners five minutes after you've known a bloke quite well. Makes you a snob, sometimes, to have your hand shaken. When he got on the bike Mark compensated by clinging to his seat behind and before him. And leaning back a bit. It was bloody uncomfortable, but outside the Bible you can't just fall on a chap's neck and kiss him.

"Don't go too bloody fast, will yah? Might miss the turn-off, see. Doubles back, and it's nothing but grass, and it's a year since I was here."

They went over the creek, stirred up a blight of brown dust, made a hell of a noise through the swamp-bush and scraggy trees, paperbarks mostly, and several carrion-crows went prophesying far inland. But they found the turn-off and lapsed back immediately into the nineteenth century, for they practically had to paddle with their feet. There was a short mile of green cart-track, overhung with lantana and roses gone back to briar, with blackberry bushes to scratch your eyes out, and parrots to shriek like witches ascending. Then you came to a boat-shed by a little creek whose whole life was only a mile long. It drew the sea-storms down from the hill, and the hill was five or six hundred feet high, and right up against the shore. Between it and the sea you could hardly have put a decent road. But here was a sheltered bank from the southerly winds, and with those roses there must have been two or three snug shacks in time past. People settled there would have had fish in the bay, and all that remarkable view to the north, as far as Crowdie Head. And yet they had tired of it. All gone. Sea-eagles, now, do the fishing off the point. Terns, gannets, dunlin and mutton-birds, they all come christening the place with their beautiful names. Mark had seen dotterel there in previous years, and the tiny little stint, sweetening the last of a wave on Lazarus Beach. He didn't know who Lazarus was, nor even if he was anybody lately.

There was still a hopeless boat in the boat-shed, with a cabin and good glass and all. You'd have thought some idle bastards might have broken it, but no. She would be rotten in the bilge, though. They wouldn't have wanted to put to sea in her.

"Just the spot," Par was saying. "But just the spot. Beaut. Bus'll like this, for sure."

He was slapping his thigh and rapping his gloves and doing a kind of sailor's caper. And then it just occurred to him,

"Like to join us? You found it. It'll be a beaut night."

"Okay," Mark said, grateful for any company.

13

It was pretty dumb of Par to issue that invitation. Mark realized it as soon as the rest arrived. He and Par went out to meet them on the Foster Road, and Mark guided them in again. But they weren't grateful. Two of them even came and said,

"You, mate, you better piss off, we're warning you."

Funny thing, it was as if they both spoke. Simple souls. They're no more courageous than a committee, are bikies. People, together, are inclined to suffer from knock-knees: knock-knees or violence. Bikies can suffer from both at once. Mark should have taken their advice, God knows, but he didn't.

There were birds around, the bikies' molls, and he was curious. He wasn't used to women who were glad to look like sluts, and no more. There were all sorts on campus certainly, and you were even proud of it, because in a university there ought to be a complete cross-section, you had to be exposed to everything. Randy women seemed to be making out that permissiveness was a sign of the scope of their brains and their sheer dignity. Mark, even when very young and ignorant, had an unswerving hunch that they were nowhere near as strong-minded as they appeared, and that they couldn't be women if they were. Therefore he was the more interested to notice the saner attitudes of the bikies' molls, for with them evidently it was all a question of heat.

For the first hour or so at the bikies' festival, everybody

was settling in. Which is as much as to say, the whole place was unsettled. Except maybe for the boat-shed and the hill, everything was milling through the darkness, even the sea and sky. Screams, curses, blankets, embraces, steaks spitted on barbecues, piles of sticks like snakes on the sand, motor-bikes coughing in their throats convulsively, beer spilling, the sea complaining. Now and again there would come up to him this teased hair and drifts of scent and red nails and giggles, like Christian evidences in persecuted places. You shouldn't be here, Mark muttered, meaning the women shouldn't, but it might as well have applied to him. The night seemed to be putting all present life at a distance, to be eerie with an older time. He could scarcely believe that he'd been so lately in Janey's house, doing dishes, counting his money, watching George ply his daily trade. Gee, he thought, not only Jesus lives, but all the past. He was aware for the first time of the real fury of the Norsemen, or, by the precarious sight of women at Lazarus Beach, under dark-ness, that he was in some gaudy feudal stronghold, where men made much of themselves, and laws for themselves, as devils try to do in the hells of their own tormenting. He should have gone.

But you don't like slinking off, and you're fascinated, as well. It stinks of its own, and you stay. In the sheer medi-eval odor of sausage grease. He thought, if he hugged the fire, it would be courteous enough to their private lives. They wouldn't blame him for knowing that, in between, they liked a mutton chop done all to ashes, or a beer. Bus himself came and was affable between chops. He had this armful of whizzbang flesh in the fold of his shoulder and a beer bottle in his left hand, but she had both arms free. Whenever he squeezed her to death, she deflected him with the chop or the boozing can. Domestic it was, such as they'd been up to every Friday night for a couple of weeks or so.

62

This Scheherazade would pass, but in the meantime she managed an air of permanence. You could feel sorry for them, if you liked, with the savage week cleaving them in two, when they might have to live apart with their parents, or if nothing quite so barbarous as that, then in some primitive single room that they never dusted, because it belonged to someone else and the rent was too rapacious for goodwill. And here they were under the simple stars, with the freedom of Cook's whole coast, and she could serve him chops at pleasure. And he could be saying (couldn't he?) in his gnomic fashion,

I will make you brooches and toys for your delight
Of bird-song at morning and star-shine at night.
I will make a palace fit for you and me,
Of green days in forests and blue days at sea.

It's the only thing for the young to say, and there must be some sad motor-cycle equivalent of it, surely? Oh, but perhaps they wouldn't bother with the brooches? Bus had wooden beads once, twice, thrice, and so had she. Anything could be gentle. But, as well, he had this bloody great buckle to his belt, yawning like a medieval gate. It must have been very sore on her navel, if she had to abide that. She wore no shield and armor, or practically none. And there was this fine blonde hair to her shoulders womanly as St. Margaret's. She shook it now and then to give a traily variety like vetch in a hedge: and to make her eyes dance behind the swathes and to bring on love.

She kept saying, "But you're so gorgeous, Bus. Do have another bite, just one. Keep up your strength, for you've a lot to do, haven't you, haven't you, love? No, no more beer, no. Because it makes you too sleepy, but far too sleepy. No, I tell you."

Courtly love, that's what it was. He had to manhandle

her to get it. And he roared the whole time to let everybody know how his loins were hurting him.

Some guy turned the transistor up and they all stomped and danced. Like something clean out of Brueghel the Elder: laughably serious with life. Certainly Bus's knees and feet, from beginning to end, paid a chaste attention to the rhythm and his thin weak mouth was almost firm. Hip and thigh he worked his queen. It is, after all, better that the world of Aquarius should also have its observances.

The tune on the transistor changed, and then the music stopped. A man started babbling about spare parts or something else essential. Mark turned to mend the fire, but after a minute it occurred to him that they had kept on dancing, through the advertisement. It wasn't much, it wasn't even strange, and yet it alerted him. He watched them most intently.

"Par," he said, "what's doing now?"

"Oh, nothing," Par said.

So Par knew of something. It was a putting-off answer. "Nothing," he said, stabbing the sand with a stick.

Par was clinging to Mark. Bus had been angry with him and given him this job of keeping his new mate close. He hadn't any moll and nobody spoke to him much. Well, that didn't make him very different. He was dumb, that was all. Flopped on one haunch, patiently at ease. It reminded Mark very much of sea-lions, who when they leave the sea are always pretending to be comfortable, poking their heads up as if they were operatic sopranos and had just taken leave of a high note. And now and again sea-lions look at you obediently as though they wished you were friends. Well, that was Par.

"You been long with this Chain Gang, Par?"

"All this season," Par said, trying to sound fixed.

"How long's that?"

"Two, three months."

"Not long," Mark said, to put him more in doubt. "You like it?"

"Course, course I do."

Par, at his job all week, could have had the bikies to boast of to his mates, and the glory of next weekend to look forward to. He might forget the disappointments then, with his mates glancing and saying to each other, "Oh, there's Bus's mate." Mark was sorry for Par. He was as near to being an outsider as Mark was himself. And he didn't know how to change it, nor whether he wanted to. Par knew that Mark was thinking him over. He wouldn't look up, kept running these little piles of sand through his fingers, or stabbing the beach with his stick.

"It's a lie, Par, and you know it. You don't like it all that much."

"It's God's honest truth, I'm telling you."

Bothered he was, cleared his throat and spit into his hole in the sand quite carefully, gave it decent interment. But that was all he did for savagery. Then he rolled on his other elbow and had to look back over his shoulder at Mark.

"Where's Bus?" Mark said.

Par just dug new wounds in the sand. Fed up, Mark took a stick and, crouching, poked it into the fire and pulled it out again to see how it was lit. Par, he saw, had his eye on the dancers and Mark followed his glance. And there, beyond them, was the Queen of the Bikies sitting alone on a rock, all hunched up, her hair like seaweed struck by lightning, with an older taste in her mouth. The dancers carried on.

"Par," Mark said, taking his stick from the fire and waving the smoke in his face, "what goes? What goes on? Best tell me, Par."

"Hmph," said Par.

"Or I'm going to find out for myself."

"It's an onion," Par said. "You maybe better split, man? That way? What say, Mark?"

Par was pointing along the rocks to Emma Beach, and he kept pointing, as though it were the road to El Dorado.

"No, no," Mark said.

But really he was thinking about this flabbergasting thing, a rape going on behind the dancing. "A rape?" he said.

"No, no," said Par in his turn, "not that. Just an onion, a gang bang."

But Mark couldn't quite take it in, found himself on his feet, trying to see beyond this mourning screen of dancers.

"It can't be," he said, appealing to Par. "Holy God." This only happens in newspapers. "Can't be." Rape's not real like this cape. "Par?" he said. "Couldn't we—?"

And he started to run. Shouldn't have. Shouldn't have done anything like that. They notice you. Running's more remarkable than rape.

There was this boat-shed with the hefty-looking boat in it and a slipway down to the sea and a cable with cranks to haul it back up, and some empty oil-cans, bagging, broken oars, the like. The slab-bark of the walls was broken in places. It was a smelly place, the way sand gets when it has been private a long time, oil poured on it, constantly pissed on. Cockroaches lurk in privy places and grow to a stupendous size. And running past, he got a whiff of all this.

On the far side there was a small group of spectators, and he immediately heard moaning going on. Par was behind him. And in the middle of the circus—

It makes you flinch a bit.

In the middle there was this dizzy licentious moaning and it excited Mark. He could see this guy on the ground, arse express, and there was a—there was writhing and struggle. You can't describe it nice. He took his hot stick, which he still had, and steered it by the spectators and right into this ass. It cracked loud out, and broke. He gave this spring-heeled start. Wailing, screaming, gnashing of teeth. Except that it was so noisy, it was all a bit like ants when you plant a foot among their goings-on. Mark wasn't sorry for planting it, but he had to be quick or be too terrified, or heaving with moans himself. It's most infectious.

The only thing was that, with those spectators—Maybe it was no worse than a bull-fight? Crowds, you've got to humor them with spectacle. But not this one, surely?

Then suddenly, in all this shouting and shoving, it dawned on him that it was Bus's ass he'd corked. He was in for trouble, and since there was no getting away, he dropped on his knees beside Bus. The girl had rolled away to attend to herself.

Bus was going on, "Oh my ass, oh hell, my bloody ass."

It made Mark anxious, but he liked the sound of it, too. And hoped it hurt.

"Wait till I get the bastard. Hell, my flipping—oh!"

"You all right?" Mark said, like a doctor, quietly. "Turn over."

He had stumbled on petroleum jelly, and Bus would have done anything then, so he turned over. Mark made soothing applications, though there and then he determined never to be a doctor. It seemed to be the way to Bus's heart.

"That's better," he said. "Much better. So long as I never have to shit again."

He turned back to his more famous side, and began deliberately breathing.

"It's you?" he said. "And how the hell did you get here? What happened? You bloody mug—"

Bus was gonna seize him by the throat, but he thought of his rear end, and gripped Mark's shoulder instead.

"Explain your bloody self."

And, of course, it was Mark that had to explain himself, not Bus. The whole mob was crowding in.

"I chased a fellah," Mark said.

"What fellah?"

"Fellah with a stick in his hand. Came and grabbed it out of the fire. And I chased him."

Some said yes, some said no. Bus couldn't keep them quiet. Some he heard say, "Par, where's Par?"

"Quiet, you guys, stow it. And what happened then?"

"He must have nabbed you, with this stick. There it is. And then — You know the rest."

"What was he like, this guy?"

"It was dark," Mark said. "A bikie. I gave you first aid," he said.

"Yes," he said. "Thanks."

From a judge, that was candid, almost genial. He wasn't too badly hurt, so long as he sat still. And it wasn't as if you could hurt his dignity. Somebody had thrust him a can of beer and he began to drink it.

But one of the dancers pushed his way in.

"Bus," he said, "I saw the bastard. He was running. And he had a stick flying with sparks. It was this bloke, sure enough."

So it was. And who else? None of them'd do a thing like that, for Christ's sake. Roast the bugger. Kill him twice. Fling him in the drink. Par, too. What about Par? Yes, Par, he should know. Where's Par?

A lot of them went looking.

"Fetch the bleeder in," said Bus, to give them a mandate for doing it.

Bus was calm by then, like a dictator with no further territorial ambitions. He cast an eye on his bare buffs.

"Fling me some pants, somebody, will you?"

And as it got calm, Mark felt the more frightened. Things were going feudal and eerie, and into martial law again.

"Where's Mary?" asked Bus, remembering in a man's world.

"I'm here," she said, almost gently.

"You orright?"

"Yes," she said, "pretty well."

Mark couldn't understand it at all, this affable selfishness in Bus. And it was a terribly terribly nice name to be raped, was Mary.

14

Although it's gnomish under the night, and crazy, too, it isn't really funny to be had by bikies on a lonely coast. They brought Par in, and they were manhandling him. He might have dug his feet in if he could, but they had his hands pinned to his back, and there were two pretty stiff-arms up at the scruff of his neck. His strides were far bigger than he meant, and it made him look smaller. Somebody switched on a headlight and they marched him right up and stood him in it. Par hung his head ashamed.

"Orright, orright then," Bus said. "Put that bloody thing off. We know it's him."

Of course Par hadn't done anything, but he was ready for sacrifice, no fight in him. He had this great ambition to be a bikie still, and he saw he was going to be disappointed of it. Maybe the only way was to die repenting that he wasn't good enough. And he was bracing himself to scream as little as possible. They sensed his co-operation and meant to make the most of it. There he stood before them. You feel misshapen with everybody looking at you: crooked through the spine and arms, one shoulder bunched up, knees nudg-

ing each other for company. Watching him, Mark was sorry
for Par, who wouldn't look his way.

There was also, for Mark, the teasing relief of being a
spectator for the moment, and of having company in
danger. He even had time to notice this thought dodging at
the back of his head: that here were the bikies acting out the
things they had seen on the screen so many times. Being the
villains that they admired for their unquestioned power
over other men, and over women like Mary, flattered by any
attention. You imitate advertisements, and think you're in
the fashion. Worse still, he'd seen a Nazi film-shot, as real as
this on Lazarus Beach. It showed you Jews arriving at
Auschwitz, herded, slow, orderly, still human. And the
camera had stopped on this blonde and handsome fellow
about twenty-four, manly, excellent, about to become a
specimen. He gave this half-amused, half-unbelieving look
around him, caught somebody's eye, and smiled. The age is
dark that we live in: but, then, it's lit by this ordinary
courage.

They went for Par first. He was their own and they hated
him.

"Well?" was all Bus said, playing him.

"I shouldn't ha' done it. I know."

"Well, well," said Bus. "Think o' that."

"I shouldn't ha' told him. It was wrong."

"What?" said somebody else.

Bus held up his hand. It was up to Bus.

"You brought 'im 'ere, right?"

"Yis."

"Ast 'im to stay, right?"

"Yis."

"To come on in, just like that?"

"Yis."

Par knew his part with a fine instinct. You come to heel.

"And you knew the rules, right?"

"Right," said Par.

"And what did you let on to 'im?"

"About there was an onion."

"But bloody hell," said Bus. "But what the hell?"

Bus almost forgot that he was the Grand Inquisitor, without feeling. He glanced across at Mark, who showed no satisfaction at human weakness, and Bus became his impartial self again.

"Why did you let on to 'im?"

"He—I think he asked me."

"You know what I tol' you? Keep 'im by the fire, I said. Keep 'im by the fire and away from what goes on. An' you said yis. You knew there was an onion?"

"Yis," said Par.

"On schedule," Bus said, very proud of it. "Eight o'clock. We timed it, on transistor. And Mary said five. Five, she said, she'd take by 8:15. We was on to a record, a bloody record, like a whole eighty guys in a telephone booth at once, and some booth too, and you ballsed it, ballsed it all up, so help me God. Take 'im aside," Bus said, "an' watch 'im. Watch 'im like hell."

He turned to Mark.

"There must be some mistake," Mark blurted out. It was—? Something dirtier than rape? "But, tell me, what's an onion? What's it, ever?"

"Right 'ere, see," Bus said, "it's me that asks the questions. An' it's you that's up for it."

And then he found that he hadn't got one handy. There was this awkward pause.

"Guy's an idiot," said Mary.

It made the court less nervous. There she was, on the ground, with her ankles tucked under her, neat like any other girl. All at once Mark felt the huge insult it all was, and out came his indignation.

"I tried to save you, Mary, and you say I'm an idiot?"

Not that he cared for being called that, or even for giving himself clean away and for the great shout that was raised at that. Caution would never carry him through, so perhaps rashness would.

"Mean to say," he said, "you wanted it? The whole football team of them? It's—perversion, not permissiveness. Why, even the trade," he said, "I mean, prostitution, it has better rules than that. It's orderly, it's well aware of morality, it's pretty civilized compared to this."

"Wot's 'ee blathering at?" Mary said. "Nattering away."

"The girls are well looked after. Doctors, police, you gotta be careful. There's umpires."

"Yah, yah, yah, you soppy big bastard. Wot you gonna do to 'im, Bus? You gonna just sit there listenin' to 'im? Lettin' 'im preach? He done you in orready, and how?"

"Look you, Mary—"

"Aw, yah, yah, yah."

Mary was braying between a man and a woman, and Mark couldn't get spoken to her, screeching bitter sayings out of the pit of her life and her acquaintance with men. Some of the bikies themselves were abashed at her.

"'Borted me kitty 'ee did. Christ, I nearly died. Me poor old gut. Ha, ha, ha, gees, ha, ha, ha."

It's an ugly world out loud, the world of sex: the bikies eased from leg to leg and cackled their embarrassment: young and rough, and now with this notion of women to carry with them through their lives, and make the future bleaker.

"I'm tellin' you," she said. "This hoof of a man. I'm all swoll and bruised. Know what I'd do wiv 'im?"

"What I'd do with you," Mark said, "is sail you away to sea. Put you on that boat, and let you go."

"Why not?" she said.

Mark was startled, mainly because he thought she meant to take him with her.

"Nobody thinks it's funny," he said, weakly.

"Why not?" she said. "But go on, Bus, why not? Him and Par, let's launch them two. They launched us, didn't they? They spoiled our date. Let 'em do each other, wot say, out there? Go on, Bus, why not?"

It didn't seem very likely. But young men out of the city, on the hop, and in a crowd, they can do almost anything. They don't know each other very well and they can't talk of mercy, for nobody wants to seem soppy.

"Hip," said Bus, and they were on to them. At least it was better than listening. Pummeled them, sat on their legs and heads, winded them properly. Someone brought a rope and cut it in two. Mark kicked and bit and struggled, but it was soon over. He was protected by their very number, but once they had mastered his legs the rest of him was pretty easy. They tied him tight, flung him aboard, and his head hit hard in the bilge and he went out, but not for long. The swish of the keel on the sand brought him to, and the whoops of the crew of bikies as they ran her for the sea, the splash of waves against the bow, the cheer men give when she's away. As best he might, he looked around for Par, and there he was, trussed up, and Mark was as glad of him as if he'd been Captain Cook.

There was a man on the bow poling her out, and one at the stern with an oar instead of a rudder, like the surf-boats. They stayed so long that Mark began to hope they were coming, too, but they weren't. As soon as she was clear of the surf they shipped their oars and poles, dived in and swam ashore to shout to their mates about it before the recklessness had all died away.

"Mark? You okay, Mark?"

"Yes."

"Gotta get out the stern oar, quick-smart. Can you?" he said.

"No, not bloody trussed up like this."

Par didn't say any more. He was trussed up, too, but he didn't even bother to mention it. Hopping, rolling, leaning, stumbling and crawling, he got there at last. His hands were tied in front of him, not to his body, like Mark's. Par had known better than to give them trouble, and they hadn't bothered themselves. There are things that other people can do, and it surprises you, but Mark liked Par for this, sitting like a galley-slave managing the steering-oar. But he couldn't see over the little cabin for'ard. The waves were on him before he knew. It wasn't really a boat to be steered as joyously as that.

"Hoy, rouse yourself, will you, you Mark? You gotta bloody well rouse yourself."

"Can't. Don't think I can."

"Can't? You just gotta, bugger it. If we're tipped out now, hell, can't even swim."

Mark nipped up at once.

"You're right, too, skipper, okay. Boy, d'you think they meant it?"

"No, no more than speed merchants, in traffic. But never mind. Just you get over here. Here, to me. *They* couldn't care," Par said. He was different now, at sea: had more words, even. "Here, grab this."

The steering-oar was under his shoulder, and with his hands he was pushing a boat-hook at Mark. Around the gunwale there was a little deck you could lean on.

"Use that, somehow," Par said. "The deck will help."

Mark got on his feet and fell on it, ankles tied and all.

"But seize this bloody hook."

"I — my wrists —"

And then the steering-oar swung to hell and the boat gave a great lurch and for the next long minute Par was cursing and going at it like Ulysses sweating it out. He'd had to drop the boat-hook and he had his hands over the oar again and he swung the boat around and kept her stemming the sea, but with a struggle.

"You orright?" he shouted.

"Yes, just about."

Mark had barely saved himself from being flung back in the bilge, but she was easier now. Par, when the wave was past, left the oar to itself, made one spring amidships, tied as he was, and it must have hurt his elbows as he balanced and steadied himself to the deck, but the next minute he was hauling and pushing Mark hard astern, like a seasick calf in a bag.

"Gee," Par said. "We don't want that again."

The oar was back under his shoulder and he was wrenching the knots at Mark's wrists unsparingly.

"But why didn't you do that up there? 'Stead of banging me head on the deck?"

"Silly question," was all that Par would say about that. He was better pleased to see Mark working the rope off his arms and chest, and over his head.

"That's better," he said. "Now me, quick-smart."

He couldn't even bite the knot, for it was on the outside of his wrists. "What a flipping thing," he said. "Good show."

He rubbed his wrists, waved them to left and right of him, chuckled, whistled, felt out of jail.

"Now we'll be right," he said. "If I'd 'a jumped and fell," he said, "we was a gonner, you know that? But now she'll be right. You can count on ten waves, the fishermen say. Some say, anyway. And we just had to count on them."

"What d'you mean, ever?"

"They say every tenth one's a big one, and we just had a big one, see? It's quiet in between, or should be. So I jumped. Lucky there isn't much surf, really, with you and me for sailors. And we still gotta get out."

"But we could swim now, couldn't we?"

"Course," Par said. "We could."

He meant he wasn't going to. He had a boat and he was skipper.

"If we could clear that low point," he said, "we could soon run her on Emma Beach. Sea would take her. I'm not too keen to make for Lazars Beach, are you?"

"No," said Mark.

You learn things about people, that you could never think up, thank God. Here was Par so helpless all day long, but now with a keel to answer him, he was the boss and you were glad of him. It wasn't in his head that the boat would founder, and very cheering it was. Pretty well always in this life, the likes of Par is a very good person to be. And Biddy, too, if you're safe ashore.

The boat lay dull on the water. She had no way except the sea and the currents. Par said the sea was coming from the south, around the great headland that shut off Fisherman's Beach with its noisier weather. The headland nosed out so far that it made Lazarus Beach a kind of grave with warm brown water, fit by day for shells in pools, and toddlers. By night, though, evil with onions and bikies, they didn't want it again. But how to get around that insubstantial rocky point? You've no chance among rocks, Par said, and Mark didn't need to be told. There's the deep swell sweeping up those rocky faults, treacherous with seaweed and all, with filthy foam and slaver and the sneering of the deep. It wasn't at all like the sand, where there was water you could subdue with your own toes. Here they were under the night with rocks in the offing, in a few fathoms of water you couldn't trust.

"She's too heavy for oars," Par muttered, thinking it out for himself. "But wait on, wait a minute. Mark, you see that oar they poled her out with?"

"Yes."

76

"Wait a minute," he said again. "See if you can find any oarlocks."

"There's no oarlocks, not anywhere, port or starboard. I can see everything."

"Course there wouldn't be," Par said, scorning himself. "I just was making sure, that's all. But you take 'em home. It's like locking up. Just look under the bow, in the kind of cabin, will you, Mark, just in case?"

So Mark looked hard and seamanlike, but not an oarlock could he find, and he make it clear to Par. Par was the best of skippers, kind and thorough, and Mark would have sailed across the sea with him, but there wasn't any oarlock.

"Okay, okay," he said, "I thought not. We're not beaten yet. You see that rope?"

"Aye, aye, sir."

Mark felt this burst of admiration. "Par, but you're a genius," he said. "One or two nights with you and I'd be a leading seaman meself. You mean—"

"Yes, but tie it on, and look sharp. On the gunwale, somehow. Won't last long. Hoigh-oop!"

It was the tenth wave, to struggle with. Lucky the oar wasn't over the side, unfastened, or it would have gone, and finished them.

Par had righted them.

"But she's drifting in," he said. "Look slippy with that oar."

"She's pointing the right way," Mark said mildly, just to show that pointing out to sea had his support for the time being.

"Can you tie a fast knot?" said Par, impatiently.

"A reef knot, yes."

"Clove hitch would be better. But that'll have to do. Be quick about it."

He was gloomy, which is a thing responsibility might do

to you. Skippers, often enough, have these slashes ploughed into their faces by despair.

"Won't last long, but it should see us through. For Pete's sake, get busy rowing. Tie it bloody anywhere, and anyhow. And don't drop the oar in, will you? God's love, we're nearly on the rocks. Stab me! To port, you silly bastard."

The damned rope was lying on the starboard side, and how was Mark to know?

"Same difference," he grumbled.

"Like hell, like bloody hell. You get her out to port this minute and pull for your life, too. Half a knot'll do."

So Mark did it quick and sat on the thwart and pulled like hell, facing him, facing the rocks so close to his shoulder. About six yards off. Par was getting ready to front them up and fend them off, where the greater danger was.

"If I shout jump," Par said, "you know what? You jump on those rocks as far as you can. Got it? The sea's no good to you here, nor the wash on the rocks, neither."

"Yes," Mark said, striving in rowing.

Picking and choosing among the waves, Par wagged his steering-oar to one side or the other, and they slid along. The dinghy on Lake Macquarie was an armchair to this. He kept saying to himself: all you know is you don't go too fast, you don't plant it deep, you don't lift it high, you skim, now pull, now easy, give a heave.

"Gee, that's it," said Par at last. "You can ease up now."

Mark lay on his oar and stared at the bilge, stared at the shore, felt blooded. The land looks steeper from the sea, looks good, looks calm with human life. Par soon turned her about, and they waited for a wave.

"This isn't a surf-board, you know," Mark said.

"Easy now, easy," Par said. "You do what I say."

And he let that wave past, and Mark waited.

"Now," he said, "give her a go."

It was keen enough, coming in on the wash, when they'd nearly been douched in the everlasting sea for good and all. It's sweet in the waves and wind, at night, and needs no other excitements. But as they drew ashore Mark thought of Lin, stemming right over the swamp, and Myall Lakes, and the mountains of the divide, to where she was, in the high country, sleeping, never knowing how they might have ended.

15

"We gotta go and get my bike," Par said.

"I suppose so, bloody hell."

It was one more thing that hadn't occurred to Mark. The boat was beached, the tide was making, the anchor was pitched halfway to the shack-shop on the hill. Mark had watched Par examining knots and oars, frayed rope, scratched paint, and said nothing.

Mark was ready to drop.

"But wouldn't it do in the morning? For God's sake, Par?"

It was the kind of mild protest that you made to your friend for life, almost a compliment, for it showed you could afford to be frank with him.

"Besides," he said, "how d'you know they won't have gone off with it? They wouldn't leave a bike about the shore. And anyway, Par?"

"What? What's on your mind?"

"D'you think they could be watching us? All the time?

As we struggled off the sea? Like the watcher angels I've read of, that look on at man's life and never make a sign, but never a bloody sign, like rock faces hewn on the edge of the desert. Par? Par, d'you think they could be back of those dunes maybe?"

"No," Par said.

Par wasn't going to be unnerved by what it said in books, but he glanced up at the dunes and he decided then and there that the boat could be left to itself. He broke into a run, and went on talking over his shoulder to fetch Mark along behind him as he made for the Lazarus end of the beach. Maybe the fear of Bus and his gang stirred him more than any eerie watcher angels, but why did he have to shout so loud, over his shoulder? And go that way at all? Mark was lively with fear of the early summer night, and the waves breaking and drowning any dangerous noises, and the silence of the dunes. All last night he'd slept on that beach and never given it a single thought.

"You see," Par was shouting, "you gotta remember how they all had to come and fetch me, don't you know?"

"Par, Par? Why're we running this way? Right into them?"

"Remember?" Par said. "When you poked Bus in the ass. And started it all. Thought I was leaving you for dead, didn't you? Didn't you? But I wasn't, see?"

"Par?" Mark called. But no.

"Course," said Par, "had I known. Had I known," Par said, "what you was going to do, I'd 've busted you first. Put a spoke in your wheel before you could put a spoke in his." Par stopped and bawled with laughter, not caring for the dangerous night. Here he'd surprised himself into a joke. "Funny, wasn't it, to do a thing like that to Bus? Mind you, it was a bit of a liberty to take. With Bus, don't you reckon? With Bus?"

Stood there, getting his breath and talking, *almost* poking Mark in the ribs. Par respected the human body and wouldn't make free with it.

"And while I was away and they were hunting me, what do you think I was doing? What do you think, eh? Stowed me bike in the bush, see, took me time about it. Thought we might just need it again, if we was fit. They won't look far in the dark, not them."

Par thought it his best move so far: cool it was, to hole up his bike.

"But by day," he said, "that's another matter. Might easily spot it. Metal, see. Gives back the sun from the bush. Can't go losing me bike. We gotta go now."

"I'm not—going near that lot. Not ever again," said Mark.

"Okay, I'll go meself. Can't sleep, anyway. Makes your ears thump, beating the sea."

"If you'd only walk," Mark said, giving in at once.

They came to the creek that bars the end of Emma Beach, and the water drains right out of the swamp, a peat-black brown, and you couldn't put your foot in it.

"Slimy rocks, too, or I might jump," said Par.

"We gotta go around, around by the road, when the tide's making like this."

"Hell, we haven't time. But p'raps we'd better?"

"It's only a hundred yards."

Mark led the way to the bridge, but on the road Par took over again. It was another world, a hinterland still as hell and unexplored, and all the more so because you could hear the surf muffling through the trees. It happens often in this continent. Two steps off the road and you're in an entangled place that hasn't moved with a human foot since time began: huge trees are hoisted above you: uncanny lives go on in ants and snakes: the whole bush blossoms and you never notice: you wonder where the birds have gone. And after midnight, crunching exposed on the road, you try not to go on tiptoe.

You hear this boobook mourning at a real slow pace: he thinks the world's been left to him. Something turns over in the long grass and the hairs of your legs are sure it's a snake. But mostly there's nothing. Bandicoots, possums, koalas, they live like gnomes behind the light, seeing you and saying nothing. And a man like Par, walking in front like a kind of corporal, beautiful with no imagination, isn't aware that life has left the district. Or Mark would think of Bus and his men sleeping at the ready, like dogs around a fire. This time they would do the pair of them in: and quietly, to suit with the bush. Silence is a terrifying thing.

"Wait on," said Par, halting.

They were creeping along the bluff between the beaches. Between them and the sea were masses of bramble and lantana with its pungent smell. Sometimes through saddles and dips they could see the line of white surf crawling up the coast to Crowdie Head, and here on Emma Beach at this time of night were two little fleeting figures running, a sandy Adam and Eve. The recklessness of ordinary life. They saw there was nobody about and they made for the boat on the sand.

"Well," said Mark, "so what?"

"Dunno," said Par. "Funny, that's all."

Here they were heading into evil and the good world was going on still, like Augustine's twin cities, the city of man and the city of God, in one and the same place, Siamese twins, incurable. Mark thought it was too bad to be permitting bikies, but those two on the beach had his permission. Love came in pairs and was beautiful.

It made him think of Lin, of course, as they edged forward in single file through the empty history of that land. Lin knew their bumpers had clicked, sure enough, and for this summer at least? Yet something put her off. Nicely set out in every bit of her from her hair to her ankles and her heels. He checked her weeping, he checked her over on the road to Cyril's garage in the morning sun, or swearing blue murder in the cause of Women's Lib, or getting on with Biddy with no age difference between them, so far as you could notice, or else embarrassed as she drove away. He knew a lot about Lin. And liked the lot of it, yes, sir.

But they were going down toward the boat-shed, better not to think of things, yet, not yet anyway. Only two days ago he'd been with her, and now these bikies. Here was midnight and mischief, the good life out at risk. He kept seeing something mocking about her eye and mouth. Par was going on, and that was silly. It was all that Mark could do to drag his feet after. Why couldn't he stop thinking about Lin? Hell, he said, you'd give her credit for anything, and you mightn't ever see her again. She's only another bird.

Came this great bloody shout from Par, waking Bus, you bet, and all his stable.

"Mark, Mark, what the devil you up to? Come on down here."

Mark ran around the boat-shed.

"All gone," Par said. "You needn't take on. Clean gone. I thought so," Par said, "and it's why I come down here first. A bit scary maybe, but it seemed empty all the time, kind of, to me. Notice it yourself?"

"No," said Mark, feeling ashamed. Ashamed of his fear, and of escape toward Lin.

But he didn't explain and Par didn't expect it.

"Now," he said, "for my bike. I wonder?"

It turned out to be a lot further back on the way they had come. Par wasn't brilliant, but he always thought sensibly. If he'd started his bike up, he wanted to know what was behind him, didn't he? Didn't want to find them all coming after, like the Vikings on the tail of the Roman Empire. They located the bike, and it was okay, and Par looked over it so long that it was tedious.

"For God's sake, let's doss down then, Par?"

"Got to get our gear, haven't we?"

But they looked and looked and couldn't find any gear, because Vikings don't leave anything behind that they can see. It was too late to get a blanket from the camp. They spent a miserable hour or two, sore and cold. If even they'd put to sea again, it might have been more comfortable. Mark got tired of going over everything to keep warm, and he said,

"What'll you do now, Par?"

What properly scandalized him was that Par had been actually sleeping. It makes you despair, to hear a strange chap breathing rough as his motor-bike. Even when he's a special pal, some of his ways will turn out to be grievous. This one, for a start. Par hadn't got below the water-table of his consciousness, because of the cold, and he kept going out like bath-water. Very depressing.

When Mark spoke, Par was on his feet in a moment, making water.

"We could mend the fire now," he said, thinking of that.

It was a thing they'd been scared to do, but privation goads you. The embers were there, and they soon had them merrily on their side. Dawn was showing in the east like a change of government.

"What'll you do now, Par?"

"Oh, home, I suppose."

"I think I'll try to get to Armidale."

"Armidale?" Par said, as though Mark had said Katmandu: probably because you need places with a beach in summer.

"Yes," Mark said, ruefully. When you're thinking of birds you've got to be careful. "Surf's not much good."

"What's on at Armidale?"

"Bird," said Mark. "Bird I know."

He made it sound in the call of duty. Par stood at the fire and warmed his hands: the first light came over the sea, bleaker than darkness itself.

Par said sadly, "Want me to take you there?"

Mark was touched and said, "Yes." He went on, "Yet you can't just do that, Par. Aren't you working?"

"It's Saturday, isn't it? You don't muck about, on a bike. Besides," he said, "I live in Newcastle, not Sydney, don't forget."

"What do you do, Par, for a living?"

"Milk-run," Par said. "It's okay, but you get sick of it. I'm with the old man. There's plenty of dough, but—"

"Oh, yes, I know. I wouldn't like to work for the old man, not at all. Mine's always in the city, never a minute to spare on anybody, it's—"

"Oh, my old man's okay. Nice guy to have a beer with, any time."

"What's wrong, then?" Mark said.

"It's not a proper trade union footing, that's all."

"Well, you could fool me," Mark was saying, but Par chipped in.

"Are we going to Armidale? Or aren't we?"

16

At first, that Thursday, driving away from Janey's place, Lin was anxious in case the Volksy would fall apart. And then what would she do? She'd been depending on Biddy, and Mark, and Janey, and liking it in spite of herself. They were nothing to her, or to each other for that matter, and yet they'd all got on well for a day or two together, all because of a broken Volksy. What she found especially peculiar was that he paid up, for she couldn't have made him, and it was a lot of money. She was ashamed to think how much, didn't like taking it, even though it was all his fault, but Biddy had said, emphatically,

"Of course you must take it."

She'd need all her own money for her sister Corrie. There wasn't much fear of her spending it only on herself. Boy friends, you had to pay for them one way or another, and probably both. Lin heard again her mother's high hysterical voice giving advice to her two daughters out of the hardness of her heart,

"Best to think of them, girls, this one, that one, every one at last, as anything fierce. Your ravisher, at least. That way you'll come to no harm."

But that was just how Corrie had thought of them, and it had brought her to harm. There was no good pretending it was joyful for her in Armidale, not now. And as for their mother, she had thought of men in different terms herself, as expendable items, but then she was married and had experience and always fully intended to be more heartless to men than they to her. It was a horrible way to grow up, to be protected with bitter words from the facts of life and then to find out gradually why there would always be some second man sniffing about the house. Her father, in the end, wandered away, expected no happiness, got divorced, married someone else. She never saw him now. But she remembered him, harum-scarum, declaring to the neighbors in his high tenor voice,

> I care for nobody, no, not I,
> For nobody cares for me.

It was a sad upbringing, full of mischief. Her mother was Isis the spider, possessive, jealous, ripe, and thinking she had proved herself the attractive one. Lin was twelve or so, and her sister eight, when her father went away. Sometimes, when she could do with help, she thought of his mop of straight yellow hair and his voice caterwauling in the garden. He had liked to call her Lindel, too. There was something gentle about him, out of his sadness. She wanted gentleness in men.

Because of the divorce, her mother was able to become irreparably respectable, married to a professor. He had a moustache with a hare lip hiding behind it. Lin's mother was German, and he'd fancied her on one of his lecture tours, and the marriage gave him scope to be European and to plan his leave in Germany. The girls were sent to boarding school, out of the way.

"Lin," Corrie had said, "I'm glad we're going to a boarding school, aren't you? We're just nuisances in his house."

"Oh, go on," Lin said. "You're old-fashioned, that's all. We could live with the prof if we liked. It's just because it's time for *me* to go, and you're tagging along."

"No, it's not," Corrie said.

Actually, you know jolly well when you're being sent to school and when you're being bundled out. There was little that Lin could say, for any comfort.

"Daddy didn't have a moustache," Corrie was saying.

"No, nor a hare lip, neither."

"Makes me shiver," Corrie said. "Like witches crossing your path."

"Suppose he can't help it. But I don't feel sorry for him. Serves him right."

"Anyway, Lin, I'm glad we're going, aren't you?"

But Corrie spoke wistfully. They seemed to be two little girls thrust out into a German fairy tale, with no hope of a fairy godmother, and the forest closing in. And they would have to manage by themselves. They'd end up, their mother always said, on her doorstep some day, babies and all, but until it happened she bore that prospect cheerfully.

Therefore, when they had left school, it was Lin and not her mother who got a letter from her sister in the hospital, written in haste and sent express, to say that she'd had her baby, a girl, and that Mike had up and left her. Up and left her, she said, underlining it. Please would Lin come at once. She was all right but she needed somebody. And Lin was best.

Perhaps, perhaps, Corrie was mistaken. Boys could do anything and not think, but maybe he hadn't sloped off at all, maybe he'd think better of it? When you weren't even half married, what then? There could be some dangerous play on the distance you went apart, and the things you threatened. Boys in that idyllic state certainly weren't looking for children, but, then, you didn't just push off and leave, not with your woman in a hospital, plus her baby. Even callousness took a little thinking out, if only to look decent in your own eyes. Driving along, thinking about it, Lin knew, for instance, that Mike's style would never have run to paying the bill for the Volksy. But maybe the bill for a baby was sort of more responsible? Or was it more irre-sponsible?

Fecklessness on both hands, was that it? Or were they really liberated, to live like this? It didn't have to do with happiness.

The prof's wife, as Lin tended to call her, would be no help now. Scintillating at some women's do somewhere, even in the morning. She'd be thinking it good enough to keep her doorstep handy. As for her dad, he never wrote. He mightn't even know of Corrie's trouble. Lin had taken up his trade of journalism and found that it wasn't for her. Too bitchy, all push. The taste of Jezebel was always on your tongue. The prof might have warned her against it, but then he—might have known better? She had refused to go to his university, where the fees were free to children of staff. Oh, well, it would have been like living on the fruits of prostitution. She was right not to go. But he would have no truck with Corrie, either, as far as Lin knew.

Biddy caught up with her, which she'd been watching and hoping for. Lin was a stranger in Armidale, though she had let Mark think it was her home once. She was glad to have Biddy to turn to as though she might have been her own mum, or, better still, somebody else's, Mark's maybe. They stopped at Muswellbrook for something to drink.

"I didn't bring him," Biddy said. "I thought it better not, in the end."

"Just as well, with this to do."

Lin tried to sound like a hard-boiled egg talking, but she had to turn and examine the other customers. Biddy was sounding her out, cautiously.

"He was quite nasty," Biddy said.

"Well, then, we're better without him, aren't we? Though I'd have liked a chance to pay him back a bit for the Volksy."

"How?" said Biddy.

They looked at each other, two women, and Lin bore the anxious glance.

"Oh, there might be some money left over, after. That's all I meant," she said.

"That's what I was hoping, too," said Biddy, "but I didn't bring much."

You fiddle with your handbag, you click it shut, you suddenly wish people would stop talking about something past and done with.

"It was only when we left," Biddy said, "that he was nasty. I don't hold it against him. He doesn't know what you're up here for, quite."

"Neither do we, do we? Let's get on with it. How about gas, need any?"

"Mind you, I did think of telling him."

"No, it's no good. I'm glad you didn't. Boys hate it when they hear of other boys running off like that. Like Mike. They think you ought to have known. Then they're vicious to you, for not knowing. As if it were your fault. And, anyway, I knew," Lin added. "The Mikes are all like this."

"Mark might have stepped in. He gave a hand with the Volksy."

"Yes, he was kind. But all she'll want is another boy friend. Corrie, I mean. Let's go, shall we? Gee, but I'm glad to see you, Biddy. I'm not bitter, really. 'Cos I know you don't need to do it at all. Thanks, thank you very much, you're very sweet."

Lin was struggling then, almost crying. She took Biddy's arm as they left the shop, and hugged it. Biddy said, for a way out of it,

"It's a good job there's women in the world, don't you think?"

"Yes. The men aren't much good, are they? Still, I don't know," Lin said, suddenly remembering her own mother.

"Come, cheer up. It'll sort out, I dare say. You're young. I must say, though, I like a man to mother. Mostly, they take any amount of it. He'll be back," said Biddy, irrationally.

But Lin thought he was as disappointing as the rest. He preferred a wave. And to put up with it all, she stared out at the windshield and fixed her mind on her driving. Girls are sillier at first, but boys keep it up longer. Oh, well, who wants them, anyway?

17

At the hospital it was visiting time, and Lin went straight to see Corrie. It was lucky to arrive in the afternoon and walk in with nobody minding in the rest of the big ward. Corrie was relieved to see her, and began at once to complain.

"Oh, where have you been, Lin? All this time? Why have you taken so long? I've been looking for you these four days. Tomorrow and you'd have missed me altogether. They're letting me out, I'm glad to say. But what a sister you are!"

Lin let her go on, pleased to see her, her brows pale with pride and motherhood and five days in bed. It made Lin feel silly for worrying all the way up: fear of the unknown needling her maybe, or only a little needless shame. Soon you could turn your carelessness around and boast about it. All that experience found out about, and a healthy baby as well. You could make a real old maid of your sister of twenty-one. And Corrie knew already, from four days of keeping company with them, that the two women in the next beds had less experience than she had, as married as they were. Sometimes she even pitied them and their dinky lives. At other times she cried a bit and was depressed and was glad of them to talk to. They just didn't know what to say, though, wrapped up in themselves, and their hubbies.

Lin sat on the bed, glad to see her sister was getting well. She'd be needing a new wardrobe now, and Lin had brought her a pair of panty-hose, and a little nylon jacket she had knitted for the baby. Corrie was pleased with her sister again.

"I'll wear them tomorrow, Lin, thank you, for coming home. I'll need something to cheer me then, and that'll just fix it. But you haven't even kissed me?"

Lin came and got a cheek to kiss, and Corrie stopped knitting her pink booties while she cheekily leaned her face. She looked very handsome, did Corrie, seventeen, without a care in the world, as comfortable as any matron with a goal scored, and ensconced in pillows.

Knowing her sister's love of herself, Lin was determined not to broach the subject of the baby, though she was dying to hear of it, and to see it, and to hold it in her arms. Biddy was on for worshipping the baby, too, but Biddy had been left in town just yet.

"And you haven't even asked to see the baby," Corrie said, at last. "But what kind of a sister are you, for goodness' sake? You're jealous, Lin. But you'll see her as you go out. The visitors troop past, just like the zoo. What do you think, even the mothers are too dangerous for the babies here?"

The evils of an orderly world were not for Corrie.

"And Mike? What about Mike?"

"Oh, that. I'll tell you tomorrow. Not here. When I get out will be time enough. And, Lin, it'll be all right if you stay in my place tonight, see, he won't be there. I've had the key for you on this table for four whole days. But it's such a relief to know how comfy it'll be tomorrow, when we come out. You're a dear, I knew you'd come."

"But—Are you sure Mike won't be there? He must have a key, too."

Lin was glad enough of the place to stay, and with Biddy, too. She wasn't staying at Mike's place by herself, for any assurances.

"Mike's gone back to college."

Mike was a student, making the time pass gaily with his car and his woman. A B.A., it was only a question nowadays of getting your ticket, as for any other trade. And in the meantime cars and women helped, for what else was there to do in Armidale? Certainly you didn't want to listen to a baby howling: that was bad for the studies. So he'd gone back to college.

"Corrie," Lin said, "I've a friend."

"You, too?" Corrie said.

"Oh no, not that. One of us is enough for that. She'll need to go to your place, too, I'll not be without her."

"Oh, that's all right. Just thought you might be growing up, that's all. Anything helps to pay the rent. Anything's welcome."

"I'll have to go now," Lin said.

She was feeling cross with Corrie and didn't want to show it, Corrie blazing the trail of motherhood for her, and cheerfully counting to be kept in dough, or bread, was it, in her lingo? But Corrie could guess what was going on, and waited, and drew Lin's eye, and said coolly, the little minx,

"It's all right, sister. You won't have it long. I'll take up with somebody else, and he'll pay his bit, and—"

"You've got a baby now. Will he pay for it, too?"

"Okay, okay, that'll be sorted out, I've been thinking.

And I'll go out to work again, you'll see. Don't preach, don't shake your head. Shacking's a way to live, you've got to understand that. We're young, and we're young only this once. It's widely done, and I'm gonna have my share."

What do you say, when fashion itself is virtue?

"All right," Lin said, refusing to look at her. "It's your life, to make a pig of."

"And Mum's?" Corrie said. "She's done herself proud, hasn't she?"

Lin declined to cope with that. Place, and money, they're always arguments, whether they make you happy or not, with the rest of your life trailing behind you.

"Bye," Lin said. "See you in the morning. We'll come for you."

"Ten o'clock," said Corrie brightly. "Thanks. You don't know where to go."

Vexed, Lin stopped where she was, for directions.

Corrie told her. "And don't forget to have a look at the baby. It's arranged."

Corrie was patting her pillows and smiling. It just occurred to Lin to stop again and ask,

"Corrie, you love your baby, I hope?"

"But sure, for sure I do."

She was suddenly anxious, with tears in her great eyes, and Lin hurried away while she felt better pleased.

And from the distance, with the baby sleeping peacefully in her crib, it was no wonder if Corrie did love the child. Lin loved her at once. All her irritation melted and left her ashamed. Everything could turn to prettiness and innocence. At one time or another, she would have to look after this baby and like it. Lord love you, but she was looking forward to it already. She wondered what would be its name, and thought how horribly stiff-necked she was not to ask. Somehow, though, she didn't think it had a name yet. It was a true defense. It hadn't.

Lin got mad again in the apartment when she and Biddy were tidying up. She was tired with all her driving, and chagrined to notice how pleased she was to have Corrie's place to come to, like coming home. She pretended to be vexed at the mess, and the whacking rent it would cost for this dingy abutment. So sanitary: concrete walls, and concrete floors, and concrete garden to keep: glass and built-in cupboards for variety. And middle-aged men making a living out of the plight of the young. But Corrie was so futile about it.

"Sitting up there," Lin said, "like Lady Muck. Propped up as though she'd only sprained her ankle. The talk of all the boys. Thinks she's in the limelight, I bet. Thinks nobody thinks the worse of her. Or the worse of her prospects in life. They can call me prim, but I wouldn't give a—a razoo for her chances."

Biddy was kind as usual, listened patiently. But Biddy could always retire. Maybe it was just an amusement to her? But that was unkind, after all that trouble, altering her program up and down. Yet if she'd known Biddy better, Lin might have stripped her mind quite bare that afternoon. It would have been a relief, to let out her own way of thinking.

On Friday morning they cleaned up after breakfast, to have everything shining for Corrie: pumfed up the cushions, hoovered the floor, made the crazy bed, cleared the sink.

"A carry-basket," Biddy said, "we'll need that. I hope she has at least a carry-basket?"

"Well," Lin said, "she has a hoover."

"But that might go with the place. It's furnished."

"She might be cadging a cot off her friends. I mean, they do that sort of thing, have all things in common and pass them around. Almost Christian."

"Well, they pass themselves around, so what's a cot?"

She looked at Lin sadly then, the older woman, blinking through her glasses.

"I'm sorry, I take it back. That sounded—off, like an old maid joking."

"You poor thing," Biddy said, getting back to whatever she was doing. "You've got such a lot on your shoulders. Unasked, too."

"Oh, Corrie asked me. Corrie asked me, Biddy."

"Never mind, you'll manage," Biddy said, thinking of her own daughter with the blue dregs of rheumatic fever about her, and an impatient husband that wouldn't make any allowances for that. "You'll manage," Biddy said.

"You think I shouldn't help her?"

"Oh, but I'm sure you should, and will, or I wouldn't be here. Yes, help her. But you're going to be left doing it. I think it's why I came. Come on, love, time we were there. We'll take my car."

Biddy gave Lin a glimpse of the pleasant life she might have had. It could be pleasant between the generations, with someone to warm to.

"D'you think—d'you think kindness is old-fashioned, Biddy?"

"Oh, no, never."

"Well, bless you, anyhow, for a kind old Biddy, to me."

Biddy was nervous at that. "Come on," she said, "let's go."

And when they got there, Matron, without Corrie's knowledge, sent for them. And Matron was inclined to address Biddy about it, not Lin, but Biddy didn't mind.

"I've sent for the baby," Matron said, "but I want to talk to you first. You won't mind my speaking frankly? The mother's young, not very satisfactory, I'm afraid. But keeping her here won't change that. Oh, sometimes she cries her eyes out, but it's about herself."

96

Lin was feeling: and why not? She's a bit starchy, this matron.

"I don't exactly know whether she understands or not. Or even cares. She could have taken a dislike to the child, after all, but I hope not that. As I suppose you both realize, this baby needs very special love, and it mightn't get it. Very special love."

"What's wrong, for heaven's sake?"

"But what's wrong, please, Matron?"

"Weren't you here yesterday?" said Matron sharply, not liking to be caught at cross purposes. "Didn't you see the baby? Oh, why are they taking so long?"

"Yes, I saw it," Lin said. "It was sleeping. It looked all right."

"But didn't she tell you?"

Lin stood shaking her head, bracing herself. Matron, to her professional credit, was agitated at her haphazard speaking. Her hands began to smoothe her uniform.

"I'm sorry," she said, "I'm awfully sorry, please forgive me. How could I suppose—but never mind. The child was born with macrostoma, too big a mouth."

"But how? What's that?"

"Perfectly healthy, except for this. The left side of the mouth hasn't formed, or been finished. It's one of those things that—that even too many headache pills could do. We don't know. The mouth continues a finger's breadth into the left cheek."

"You mean she has a mouth and half?"

Matron nodded. "That's it. She's had a lucky escape. Could have been cleft palate and hare lip, but it's not. There are side effects, too. Little excrescences near the ears, and in the middle of this cheek. Oh, thank God."

The baby was coming. Hare lip, Lin was desperately thinking. Was that why Mike was so quick to move away?

But he was wrong, surely? They say a hare lip is hereditary, but you wouldn't get it from your step-father, good God?

18

Here was the baby come to save them all, as babies will with women. Broken and contrite noises, over this gnomish infant, what else could they manage then? Lin thought how this little thing was her own kin and she would love her. This very fine delicate face she had, till she opened her mouth and cried. Cried herself back into an early world where she would have been exposed on the mountains or eaten in time of drought. Cried like some frog god taunting human beings through a baby's face. But these were wounding thoughts to have? She couldn't help it. And she couldn't take up the baby, either, and hug her and hug her till they both felt better. But what were they to do?

Matron certainly was most kind, went over all the business of feeding once again. As a gesture of relief, she was glad to, though she had already told Corrie once or twice. They were to hold her cheek closed or, poor thing, she wouldn't be able to suck, and she'd take in far too much wind. For the rest, they were simply to treat her as a normal baby, which she was. Dr. Forbes had given her a thorough check and she was as perfect as anybody else. They hadn't to think anything bad about her, Matron said, for she was a very sweet baby, wasn't she, and they'd all have to wait and see what the professors in Sydney said. Matron had never met this before, this macrostoma, but they'd met it in Sydney, she knew for sure, and they would do something. Dr.

Forbes said there was only one man for this operation in the whole of Australia, and that was Dr. Pretherick. But whether the op would be done now, or when the cheek was better formed —

"But could the cheek be better formed?" asked Lin. "There might be some gristle missing."

Matron just went on and finished. "Or when the baby is stronger, or when she is twelve or so." Matron smiled. Certainly she was firm and kind.

— But twelve or so! All those years at school for a little child, with everybody curious and scornful. All those wounds of the spirit. Kids calling after her, that should have been her little friends, giggling, nasty, foolish. Oh, no, no, no, not that. Too cruel for anybody to suffer, far less a little girl, and pretty-natured. Lin looked at Biddy and burst into tears and turned away and Matron had to stop. Matron was upset, too. What's more, she was glad to see those tears.

"Whatever is for the best, dear," she said, "I'm sure it will be done. You're not to take on. My goodness, what they can do nowadays: we're lucky to be living now. We're all so grieved about it. She's such a good baby, such a bright wee thing, and pretty, really."

They got away. Corrie was saying thank you in a practical voice. There was a carry-cot in the back seat beside Lin, and the baby lying on her left cheek with a dummy in, to make her practice sucking. Two nurses were shutting the car doors, Matron still hovering about. It was royal treatment, or else it was simply the country, which is courteous. Anyhow, all they could do was to wave goodbye and stand aside. Wishing wouldn't mend it. But they waited till the car turned out of sight before returning to their daily business.

"Well," Corrie said, "what do you think? Gee, I'm glad to be out of there."

"This is my sister Corrie, Biddy."

"And nice of you to come for me, too. Having a new kind of holiday, are you? Your car? Or Lin's? Need all the help we can get, my baby and me, and then some. But I'm grateful. Not much of a world for a girl on her own, is it? And the things they do to you in there. I'm all black and blue. And, gee, those paper diapers, they're not so good, are they? You still need cotton ones. Any good at washing diapers, sister? You'd better be, to show me."

It was Corrie's day, and somebody had to talk. Biddy had suddenly become a most intense, slow driver, studying the traffic, unable to notice much that Corrie said. Corrie picked out friends of hers on the pavements, and waved, and obligingly told Lin their recent history, some of it scandalous.

It was the landlord that broke Corrie down. They were sitting in her apartment drinking tea, and the baby sleeping, nothing on the move. Apartments, very often, are built in these low places in Armidale, where they first lay a concrete peninsula into the fields, and some of this desolate concrete becomes half a dozen living-room floors, with tiny bedrooms abutting, and the plumbing at the front doors taken under the rest of the concrete, where the cars come to a halt. There's a glass wall looking on the fields, with a french door, but you can't use it much, because of the blow-flies. Cattle stray across your curtains, Jerseys or Guernseys, neat and gentle creatures. That summer, because of recent rain, the grass was green and fresh. You could see the dregs of the weather in the lumps of clay that the cars brought in and left in brutal parcels among the clotheslines. It was touch and go country, where if you looked one way you were in the town, and it was the only way that Corrie looked, as she had a perfect right to: toward the corner store and the sprouting garage opposite, and one day curbs and gutters would come, and they'd be wholly civilized. The trees would retreat, and the magpies, and the song of the butcher-bird. Still, you must have food in cans, and Rice Krispies. And when you have a baby, you're for ever trekking to the shop, so it's just as well if it's handy. It should have been an idyll to live there, but it wasn't, for the landlord came.

"I don't intend to muck about," he said at once to Corrie.

The apartments were not unlike a railway carriage, with him at the door, ticket-collecting when you'd got none. One thing, it was Friday morning and perhaps there was nobody in the next roomette. There has to be full employment in apartments or how could they afford the rent? Besides, in late November some of the shacking students would have gone home. Maybe the landlord had his own problems.

"Been talking to Mike while you was away, and he tells me it's all up. Well, it's no skin off my nose and I'm not even curious: just that the wife nags at me something awful. She likes the rent coming in, though. She ain't too moral about that, I'll say that for her. Course, hope you'll do all right, and that sort of thing. You'll find a place, you'll see, and this here's no good for babies."

Corrie was going to say something then, but he wouldn't let her. Just raised his voice.

"But they're too small, these places, see? You know that. I'd just like the key tomorrow, thanks, if it's agreeable. All paid up and proper, Mike saw to that. Good bloke, some ways, Mike. Pity if you can't make a go of it, the pair of you. I like to see young folk nice and settled now, I do so. But I reckon it was Mike as I was dealing with, no? No niggle-niggle, higgle-haggle. No, I won't look in. You been okay by me."

He saw there was company, and he wouldn't want to take on three people, all women. Not when money was the name of the game.

"But," said Corrie, "I'll get my job back, and Mrs.

McGonagle, you know her? She says she'll mind the baby and—"

"I'm very glad to hear it, love, very glad. And you'll get somewhere else all right, you'll see. It's just that these places are small, and there's others to think of, and you know how it is."

"But you can't—"

"I gotta go now. Told you in the first place the apartment wasn't for kids and you swore black and blue there was none coming, the both of you. Well, Mike mightn't ha' known, but it's none of my biz. I'm not saying he did or he didn't. Gotta live, that's all. There's no sentiment in this inflation, or the bloody taxes, I'm telling you. One thing about students, they change quick with the terms and you gotta be up to it. But as well, they fancy this shacking and it's good for business. Don't know what we'd do without the university. It's not me as invented it, lady, not shacking. Tomorrow, if you'd be so kind? And don't worry. Try Mrs. McGonagle's, if I were you. Might suit you both. She could have a room."

They'll not only kick you out, but give you advice, too. Corrie slammed the door in a great tizzy and the baby started up.

"What'll I do, oh what'll I do? Better go and see Mrs. McGonagle right now. Or d'you think I should go and see Mike? Oh, no, I know that's no use, oh, dear, oh, dear. Me and my baby, what'll we do? Lin, what'll we do? It isn't my fault, is it? It's the men, they don't care, if they can bed us. And I'm not going, I'm not going, hell. He'll have to come and throw me out. He can't do that, can he? I'll bite his bloody ear off, see if I don't. They can put me in jail. Wish I was back in the hospital, even."

Biddy was trying to quieten the baby, but without success. Lin kept turning Corrie's way as she hopped about, newly out of the hospital, easily hysterical. At last Corrie flung herself on the bed and burrowed around and sobbed and sniveled and blew her nose on the sheet, and was easier after that. Biddy wanted to take the baby up, but wouldn't because it wasn't hers, and Lin did it for her, flinging her over her left shoulder to pat out the sobs and burps and say, There, there. It was good to be doing that, walking about with a real baby that grew to you and settled quieter and quieter.

"She's almost looking already," Biddy said. "She'll be a smart one, I bet. There, yes, it's my glasses, sweetheart. Shiny-shiny. Yes, love, everything's all right, no cry."

Just anything Biddy was saying, and smiling, and Lin liked her the more for it.

"Now I'll warm up her milk," said Biddy. "You don't give her too much, but there's nothing wrong with her appetite, is there? Oh, dear, oh, dear."

Something had upset Biddy, and it surprised Lin, on top of those wooings and cooings. Lin lifted the baby off her shoulder and she made to cry again and there was this great gash across her appearance, and those little fleshy excrescences beside her ears, and Lin was soon as bad as Biddy. Four girls, all near crying and desperate. But she clutched the baby to her again and said in a Big Bear voice,

"You're a darling, aren't you? We'll see this right, you and I. And I'd like to see who'll stop us. Darling, that's you. It's all better."

Corrie was sitting up on the bed, dreaming or sulking, or something in between. Comfortable, one hand up and down her thigh, she was stroking herself back to content. But she saw Lin watching her, and roused herself.

"Still might come back?" she said. "If only he'd given me about another three days, that landlord, old so-and-so."

She was kidding herself about Mike, for all Lin knew, and

it didn't seem of first importance, anyhow. She kept on walking and crooning. Daisy, Daisy, gimme your answer, do. I'm half—

"You don't have much chance to work on them in hospital. The boys, I mean. And I'm used to this flat. I like it. He likes me well enough."

—crazy, all for the love of you.

"Can't do much at the weekend, can I? What's the time?"

Biddy came with the bottle, then, and Lin didn't answer. It was about eleven, or a bit later. Corrie's words themselves were only so much day-dreaming, but there was also this smile and this stroking. As though she were stroking her memory. And when she lay back on the pillow with her hand behind her head and her bust all braced and her eyes on the ceiling and drew up her leg and breathed so vastly and rolled her head and smoothed her skirt on her recovered inside, with this athletic smile and sighing, it wasn't very hard to follow Corrie, with the notion of a man back in her nostrils. Young girls were still alive, after their babies came: and whetted. It provoked Lin: and it provoked her to admit she was provoked, too.

"Well. There's more fish in the sea than ever came out of it, isn't there? Well, isn't there?" Corrie said, raising herself on one arm. "We can't all live as dreary as you."

It was commonly talked over among Corrie's friends, so obvious. And it would be a triumph, too, to make Lin admit it. She hadn't a body for nothing, even Lin.

"Yes," Lin said, "there's fish, but why should they be for you?"

"Oh, you'll see—"

"What's more, you've netted your catch."

"—that boys are like flies—And what's that?" Corrie said.

"This baby."

104

"You can have her. But only for a bit, for a bit, I said. Gimme her. She's mine. I love her."

"Oh, Corrie."

Corrie was maybe thinking to give this baby away? Well, and maybe it was the best thing, too? But who would have her? And balanced against the man trade, just like that, it was crude enough. No wonder she gave off some display of affection.

"I'll feed her myself," Corrie said, defying them, putting them in the wrong, as though her battle were with Lin and Biddy.

"Corrie," Lin said, "why did Mike go away? So suddenly?"

Corrie didn't look up from her feeding, but the baby missed, and cried. She had to grip that cheek together again.

"Don't you know?" she said. "You that's so good at guessing."

"No," Lin said. "I've never seen him."

"Well," said Corrie, and paused, and glanced at Biddy. "I can't help what he thought, can I? It was this lip, he said. Suppose he didn't like the look of it. His mates, somehow. Might scorn him, I dunno."

"Might scorn him because of this poor baby?"

"He said they would. He did, Lin. Don't be so innocent."

"And the hare lip?"

Not that it was a hare lip, but the question drew Corrie's eyes defensively and she was nodding and excited.

"Yes, that hare lip. Mike said they were hereditary," she said. "Yes," she said, "he wanted an excuse."

Biddy was blank enough, knowing nothing about the family, but Mum's professor with his trim, incestuous moustache was standing there between them, and what had they to trust in, either in him or in Corrie's way of life? Your life, somehow, gets the blame that it deserves.

"Oh, Corrie, Corrie, but say it isn't true? You didn't have any affair with him, did you—not with Professor Croll?

Corrie, with the glitter of experience in her eye, left off looking at Lin and held her baby up and kissed it on the proper cheek, and said,

"She looks all right, doesn't she?"

She was always inclined to fend off her sister's stuffiness.

"But say it isn't true?"

"All right, and I did, of course, but—"

"Oh, Corrie, but what, but what?"

"He wanted to believe it. It gave him the chance of a change. Changes are lightsome, aren't they? Oh, go on, Lin, I think they are, too. It's just that—You've got to get in first." She looked again at her baby, kissed her again. "Haven't you, darling," she said: hugged her, held her up, made another kiss in the air.

Then she hastily passed the baby to Lin and was off to the bedroom, shutting the door. Poor Corrie was more desperate than she could afford to look, whichever way it was, and whoever was the father of the child, and who could care to measure the difference? Not Lin. Heartlessness is such a stone inside everybody, that's all. To treat others as though they were things, it's the way of the sexual world, and we've all got it. And you can't turn your back and still go on loving, whether you're Lin or Corrie. Lin knew that, at least.

Next day Corrie said,

"Oh, there's one thing I know: I can't leave this town till they tell me about Dr. Pretherick. And if he wanted to see the baby next week, even Mike and the landlord wouldn't want to shove me around, would they? Dr. Forbes might get a reply today. I'm going up to the hospital. Don't let him put us out till I get back."

She was running around titivating as she spoke.

"I'll take you," Biddy said.

All night they had been turning things wretchedly over and over. What both Lin and Biddy saw, of course, was that they had to keep near that baby. Biddy had been no spectator. The sisters looked to her. And Corrie would have to go to Sydney with them, very likely.

"But the baby mightn't have to go in years," Corrie kept saying. "What do we know about it?"

Lin kept worrying about the two cars, and all the money of it, and the suitable baby food, and whether her place in Sydney was big enough for the new family there now was: and how Corrie's ways would take over her ways, in Sydney or Armidale. And Lin herself would have to go out to work, and come home to her own place and find herself a stranger. Boy friends might be coming and going, and Lin (she struggled against it, but couldn't win) suspected Corrie's boy friends of plying her like a cigarette machine. Corrie already had the bitter taste of nicotine about her body. Love shouldn't be as sad as that. No Mikes for Lin. She wasn't at all a prissy person, but she was looking for a boy that would do more than dish her, if there must be four-letter words. It's not uncommon yet, her attitude.

And while they were away at the hospital, and the baby sleeping, there was this knock at the door, and Lin thought it would be the landlord. But it was Mark all grinning and smiling.

Lin was pleased, and ready to cry, but Mark saved her from that by introducing Par.

"And how are you getting on?" he said then. "And where's Biddy?"

19

It's a rough road to Armidale, a road like the kick of a
horse. Somebody ploughs up a piece of the desert and instead of blossoming like the rose it falls into a succession of
bloody great holes. Every twenty yards or so you find yourself bidding goodbye to the earth, like Elijah with Elisha on
the back wheel, and of course you leave the whole world
behind you lousy with dust. There's glimpses of natives,
hats crushed on the back of their heads, conducting themselves in Governor Macquarie's time, or in paradise, for it's
a helluva halo these bushwhacker hats have. Then all at
once, at Bendemeer, civilization comes on again, and there's
trucks galloping at sixty miles an hour and the edge of the
road is strewn with dead parrots, that have come to feed fat
on the grain that drops off. It's a pity, for they're prettier
than trucks. Wiser, too, for that matter.

By the time they reached Armidale, Par was so much the
skipper again that he insisted on knowing the way to the
hospital, though Mark could see he didn't. It's a peculiar
sign of being all male, and Par had it. Women will ask the
way, even when they're right on it, especially if they have to
stop in the middle of the road, suddenly. But Par would
keep on playing at Tic-Tac-Toe with Armidale, because it's
laid out in squares, and people keep killing each other at the
intersections. After a while, instead of murdering the other
bloke, or just cursing him, Mark yelled out,

"Hospital?"

The other bloke blinked and leaned out of his window.

"Yes," he shouted, "better give yourselves up. Keep on driving like this, and you'll soon be taken."

His teeth burst out then. He wasn't angry, just a learned man from the university. Facetiousness made Mark sure of that. But they gave him a wave of thanks and Par began to explain what had foxed him, and it lasted till they got to the hospital.

Biddy was there, but they didn't run across her. At the inquiry desk, the girl was suspicious, and didn't want to give the address of all the newborn babies in Australia, in case they were a couple of Herod's troops. And then Mark remembered that the name would be Jamieson, and the girl was still suspicious, but she knew who they were at.

"We're not baby-farmers," Mark said. "Oh, come on."

"I know that," said the girl. "But you might be in the industry, just the same."

"What industry?"

Mark didn't get it, though he knew it was off-putting. She was a pretty girl, and he showed his appreciation of that all the time, to help co-operation. Then he blurted out,

"Oh, it's not the mother of the baby. It's the sister I'm looking for. I've come up from Sydney, with my mate."

She was ashamed of her mistake. She had thought them lovers of the wrong sister, and she gave them the address before she realized to herself that it was much the same whichever.

"Oh, well," she said, out loud, "what's it matter?" And she went on with her work, vaguely disappointed with herself. "Two bikies, that's all. And their molls, I suppose." And later still she said, "And we do the sweeping up."

Mark, on the other hand, when Lin opened the door, was genuinely pleased. It wasn't everybody that had his luck, setting off up the highway looking for a wave, ramming a car and a boat and the tail-end of Bus, and fastening on three good friends, and shoring up in the mountains, four thousand feet above the sea, and all in one week. He'd write home at the weekend and tell them some of it. Sooner or later they'd have to get used to Biddy, and Par, and Lin, yes maybe Lin. There was a ton of girls that they might like to know, but you couldn't have the whole ton: you had to choose. They might have to be content with Lin some day. Anyway, he'd write home, for she'd be worrying, that was Mum.

"Par's my best friend," Mark said, "except for you and Biddy, and it's time you got to know him. What have you been doing all the week?"

Lin shrugged. "Well, the Volksy's chugging away, thanks for asking."

"That's good. Oh, Par has a headache and so have I after all that road. Got any aspirin, please?"

"Yes," said Lin. "Come in, but you'll have to be mighty quiet. Excuse the mess, of course."

Par was plain shy of girls and clumsy in the presence of new ones. Lin liked him the better for it, but made no sign or fuss. He sat down, hoping his manners would be adequate till they all got accustomed, and that Mark wouldn't pull his leg. And, taking his cue from Lin, Mark didn't. Par had suddenly assumed that he'd become of no importance, and it wasn't like that. Lin knew how to cheer him.

"I'll make you some sweet tea, and then give you an aspirin."

They felt sure that would be right. A woman doctor is half the medicine, and the better half at that, especially if she's in the family. And Lin spoke up as she switched the pot on.

"Par, don't tell me he's just conned you, too? How did it happen, ever?"

Par smiled. "Spoke to him on the beach, you know. My fault. Showed me how you go for Lazarus Beach and we spent the night there."

"Well, most of it, on and off," Mark said.

"Good mates after that," said Par. "Hope I—ain't done wrong, bringing him here, you know?"

He was keeping off the boat journey. It could wait.

"Oh, no," said Lin quickly, "it's not wrong. He makes friends a bit soon, that's all. And I might as well warn you, he even keeps them, I think, though I don't know why. Your bike's not your own, after. Everything's changed."

"It's how I feel, too," said Mark, taking it all.

But Lin ignored him.

"You weren't coming to Armidale at all now, were you? Be honest."

"No, I wasn't," Par said.

"Oh, there's the baby crying."

Impulsively, she dived into the bedroom, brought out this baby roaring, with the ugliest great crack across its cheek, and held it up to Mark, defiantly, for him to take. And he was cut to bits: on his feet, not wanting it, hands flopping, passing his fingers through his hair.

"Oh, Lin, what a—I can't, might drop it."

But Lin wasn't really giving it over. His hands fell away.

"See," she said, "that's what. I told you not to come among us."

"Oh, Lin," Mark said, "the poor thing. Is it—? Can they mend it?"

He didn't know whether it was a man's business at all, and yet he knew that she was testing him in some way.

"But what a tragedy," he said.

He tried looking over at Par, but Par hadn't been allowed to see it yet.

"And how do you get used to that, my friend?" said Lin,

quite cruelly. "Harder than a Volksy, isn't it, to get used to? And what are *you* to do about it, Sir—"

She was going to say, Sir Galahad, but her vehemence betrayed her. The pot was boiling over and she paid no heed. The question pulled him in and out of her affairs. She bit her lip, didn't stay for an answer, but rushed back into the bedroom and slammed the door. It was Par who switched off the pot.

"Boy, it's a worse hole than last night, far worse. Boy, oh boy. But what do we do now? I hope Janey's kid'll come better than that. Gee, it isn't fun, after all?"

"I'll make the tea," Par said.

Mark could see that it wasn't his affair. It was women's work, like boudoirs and seraglios. Maybe they shouldn't have come. And yet again, maybe it was the place where a family came in, where you needed to be a family. It's a good rule when you're twenty that there shouldn't be any babies about. He didn't know any more about the world than this baby.

"I'm sorry, Par, for lugging you into this."

"Oh, I don't know," Par said, cheerfully.

"Might as well be a bikie. They've smaller problems."

But Par shook his head, and it pleased Mark.

"What's up with the kid, now tell me?"

Between them, they were pouring out three cups of tea.

"It's got this gash in its left—no, wait a minute." Mark moved around to face himself. "Yes, this gash that travels into its left cheek. As though the devil had been at its brewing, and taken scissors, and cut in. Just like that, a cruel thing. Poor kid. But it's no business of yours nor mine, Par, nor of Lin's, either."

"Gawd," Par said. "Can't anything be done about it?"

"Yes, can't anything be done? Gee, you don't reckon on the likes of this, do you, when you're having fun? It's not in

112

the rules, is it? It's a thing for the parents, though: they can put it right."

"And the oldies," Par said.

"Yes," said Mark, "of course. Don't know if there's any oldies here, except Lin."

It seemed to them sad as well as strange. Mark thought how warm and hearty Par's father must be, the milkman, that lived all night behind society.

"Let's go and ask her," he said.

The baby was howling, but at the door there was this sobbing, too. Mark, a bit uncertain, looked over at Par again, but he was pretending to think as he sipped his tea, as if he'd quietly become a solemn person, like a Member of Parliament. Mark knocked and opened the door. Lin and the baby were strewn on the bed like a beaten town. He sat down beside them and put an arm around Lin and crept in closer, but she flung him off. They both sat up with their necks broken and scratching their heads. Par came with a cup of tea for Lin.

"Thanks, Par."

She made no move to take it, twiddling her tiny bib of a hankie, hitching her tiny bib of a skirt around a place where it wouldn't go, sniffing.

"I'll just put it here if you want?"

Par put it on an attentive chair, precariously.

"Thank you."

She blew her nose.

"I'm sorry," she said.

"It's okay," Par said, "I've a sister, too."

As if it explained everything. Mark said nothing, but he was inclined to wag his leg annoyingly. Lin put out a hand and stopped him, looked up, gave a wan smile.

"Sorry," he said. "Wasn't thinking."

But he was. He was thinking how you've got to see a bird

113

at home with her wings off before you know what she is, a part of the ordinary day. And it's a strange pleasure that, for it draws you, in its weakness. The boys went and tidied the sink, for something to do: talked about spoons for a change, and the scalding of baby bottles. Nobody mentioned aspirin, till Lin remembered, and called from the bedroom. No, she wouldn't have one herself.

Biddy and Corrie came in, and once again the place was full of talking.

20

There's a clear logic in the trouble you take, especially with Biddy giggling. Mark and Par had come all the way from Lazarus Beach, and Corrie saw her advantage at once.

"I see," she kept saying, "you're Lin's boy friend, are you? So you're Lin's boy friend? How come I wasn't clued up? But it's just like you, Lin."

And Lin was saying, "Oh, boy friend nothing. Trust you to think of boy friends. Oh, rubbish. He's just a boy I met. Or bumped into. Why should I tell you? Fat lot you tell me till it's too late."

Lin had forsaken her sobbing and was on the rampage with diapers, pots, and safety pins. Biddy had pulled up her skirts and had the baby raw and kicking on the rampart of her knees.

"Tut, tut," said Biddy, to Lin whirling about, "you're upsetting the child."

Corrie was free then to ask what she liked, but at last Lin cut in again.

"What did they say? Any news? Yes, from the hospital, what else?"

"Oh, that. Yes, we've got a date next week."

"On Wednesday," Biddy said. "I can take the two of them, if you like? Was going back anyway."

"Where is it, then, this date?"

"Sydney, of course. Children's Hospital. Professor, surgeon, they'll all be there. To see my baby. But—Why, oh why should it happen to me? Don't rouse on me, Lin. You've got to help me, please."

"Well, we're here, aren't we?" Lin said, not very struck with Corrie's collapse.

For Corrie had flopped on a handy box, and spread her limbs like little orphan Annie, and made her legs as sweet as she could for the sake of the two fellahs in the room. Lin stopped and sized her up, jealous, uncomplimentary.

"I can see you'll be all right," she said, going on again.

But Mark must have kept looking at Corrie a fraction too long.

"Don't be taken in," said Lin, sharply. "Or else, be taken in if you like. You have my permission."

She sounded much as she always had, as if she expected, at any time, that he'd just get up and go. Lin saw very well that in days of Women's Lib it wasn't only the women who were free: but it was still the women who got hurt. And so she was defensive from the very start.

"You see the Jamiesons at their best," she said. "Struggling in the troubles they make. There's plenty more if you keep coming."

"Lin, Lin," Biddy was saying, "it's not like you."

"It is," Lin said, not able to shut her bitterness up. But then she was sorry and said no more.

Corrie was sweet and sisterly, saying nothing, smoothing her stocking. Biddy got up and commandeered the floor, rubbing the baby's back till it brought on a feast of burps and loud applause and other light relief. Lin was desperately folding diapers, and when that was done she took the pot and spent ages scouring it in the bathroom, not shutting the door to be unfriendly.

"Mark," said Biddy, "I want to speak to you in a minute, when the baby's down. It's about the A40."

"Oh, but Par's better at it," Mark said.

"No, not Par. It's you I want."

"Well, he can help anyway."

"No, he can't."

"I'll take the baby," Corrie said.

None too pleasantly, and quite without a word, Biddy handed her over. But Corrie just crooned and was her own sweet self and picked the shawl off the baby's face, smiled, rubbed noses, kissed the baby.

"Come on," said Biddy to Mark, unaccountably angry.

"Back in a minute, Par. I'll call you, if I need you."

"Mark," said Biddy, lifting the hood, "there's nothing wrong with this engine. You can help, see, or beetle off."

"But—"

"You can help or beetle off, I say. That's all. There's nobody looking for a wave now. That poor girl's got plenty on her shoulders, and she takes it very well. I know. I've watched."

"Who? Corrie?" said Mark, deliberately, for he felt he hadn't earned this ticking off.

"No, of course not. Lin. She's torn to bits. And if—. Life's serious, Mark, and I'd like you to help."

"Okay," Mark said, "I will. Why d'you think I came? We've had our troubles, too."

"They're nothing to this. And Lin can't see how to sort it out, or if she should. We'd better go back. Let's go."

And as they walked back, Biddy added, more mildly, "It's the baby, you see, entirely the baby. Lin's fond of her

116

young sister, you can be sure, but she wouldn't interfere if it weren't for the baby. She's needed."

The landlord came, and saw the boys.

"These two come to help you flit?" he said in his despair.

There was this leap of resentment at them all for being young, although Biddy's presence should have comforted him. But when you know that there's fornication outstripping you every day, you retire into the dignity of your envy. You disapprove and draw the rent. This man had put his life's savings in apartments, to find himself a kind of a peeping Tom. They copped it for Mike and his kind, and yet, what's more, the landlord had some sympathy for Mike, had been talking to him.

"Oh, well," he said, "when the baby wakes, but that's it. Finish. I been kind to you. Tole you yes'day, didn't I, gev you time? An' wot do you do? You stuff the place up wiv two more men. You don't do that wiv me. After lunch, as quick as get-out. Never mind about cleaning up. You been no trouble, but there's the rules, see? You know there's no kids, can't have that, lady, can't have that. There's next door to think of, always. Gas and electricity I won't check it, for it's been done recent. Leave the key in the lock, will you?"

Casual, that's what. But it gets business done with a minimum of fuss, and nobody's hurt if you just carry on.

"He wants to put somebody else in," Corrie said. "As if we didn't know. And the rent will go up. I wonder who?" she said, with a sudden thought.

Mark and Par bundled everything into the cars, which were none too big for what there was, with three women and a baby. And yet the apartment was supposed to be let furnished. It's women that have the acquisitive instinct, Mark thought.

"But I wonder who's coming in?" said Corrie every now and again, not helping much.

"Anyway, Corrie," said Lin, "what does it matter? We've got to be in Sydney next week, well clear of this."

"Yes, but I've got to go somewhere in the end."

"Oh, well, we'll see about that."

They were out by ten to two, and the key was in the door. Two cars and an escorting motor-bike, so that it all had a kind of stateliness, perhaps. Just as Corrie was getting into her seat, she stopped and stood. It's a thing that married women are inclined to do, while everything else hangs on its hinges.

"Oh, there's a roadside stand beyond the airport, on the left. Could we all stop there, do you think? Just in case we come to and remember something, that we might have left. And there's things to get. At the stand."

"What things?" said Lin, at the wheel, impatiently.

"Fruit, veggies," Corrie said, kindly. "Might be glad of them in Sydney. They're cheaper."

"Might get some, too, then," Biddy said.

Lin shrugged, but when they drew up at the stand, her suspicions returned. She was driving Corrie and the baby, and Mark was driving Biddy.

"Oh, Par," Corrie cried, so apologetic that she was almost yelling. She had to cry over the motor-bike, which Par was revving in his proud professional way. "There, it's just as I thought it would be. D'you think, Par, you could please go back for a pair of shoes I've left? I'm very sorry. I'll tell you where they are. They're under the sofa. Can't think why I missed them. Sorry, Par."

Par was important and delighted. What do you have out-riders for? He was off before he'd bought a single vegetable, and Corrie didn't know what the hell to buy either, nor had she any money. It was Biddy that laid waste the stand, bought a whole haystack of stuff, and then had to sit with her feet among it.

118

"Why do you think she did that, the little minx?" said Biddy, as they moved away.

But Mark was driving grimly. Women would provoke you, with their lost shoes and abundant vegetables. If he'd been Par, he'd have told her where to get off, for sure.

But it turned out that she knew what she was at. Par came roaring back with a catch of shoes, and he was just going to brandish them and pass on, to reassure them, but Corrie stopped Lin's car and was determined to get them.

"She's not gonna let Par drop them off," said Mark, grimly, "but damned if I'm stopping. Not again."

"I knew he'd find them, of course," said Biddy, looking back.

It was only after they had stopped for tea and started again that Biddy tackled Mark.

"You've no curiosity, have you?" Biddy said. "You haven't that much sense. The new tenants were in the place, and that's what Corrie thought. And who do you think they were?"

"How should I know, in all Armidale?"

"Mike and his new woman," Biddy said. "And well in-stalled."

"No," said Mark, flinching off the road. "Couldn't be?"

It's a funny crude old world.

"Think we should go back and job him?"

"I think we'll just carry on," Biddy said. "'Tisn't new. It's just a hippy thing to discover it all again. Springs out of sheer unhappiness. Is a recipe for it."

Soon, for Mark, too, it became a bit of ugliness they could really do without, something that would only hinder them. He wasn't even very sorry for Corrie, because she'd asked for it, and yet in a wispy way he maybe grieved for her, as they drove along. They were an odd family in unfamiliar places, pretty vulnerable. And already Par and he had had enough of driving for one day. Where were they all to stop for the night? The roadside might have done, but not for Biddy, not for the babe.

"We gonna stop for the night? Or just push on?"

"Stop," Biddy said.

There's one thing about women, he thought, they may keep changing their own minds, but they know what everybody else is going to do.

"You mean now?"

"No, for the night. We set off far too late, do everything badly. But if you live this way, oh dear, you've got to expect disadvantages, I'd say."

"For a scratch team—"

"Oh, yes, I'm sorry, for a scratch team we might do." She leaned over and patted his knee. "You're a godsend, you two. Coming in from the hospital, it was something to see you all right. Like losing a pound or two. I don't know when I was so glad. Things took a turn then."

"But Lin isn't all that pleased, is she?"

"Yes," said Biddy, "she's pleased. How could she be pleased, with all this on her hands?"

It was a funny answer, both ways.

"I suppose not," Mark said, doing his best to like it.

"You've gotta be careful, Mark. You went out looking for a wave and just look what you've bought into."

"I'm not complaining, though. Waves aren't better than women. Though there's all kinds, right here. One of them would do: you, Biddy."

Biddy giggled at that. You drive along, stare through the windshield, pepper it with sad little phrases. Nobody says much. If they're good friends, that is.

"We'll stop at Tamworth for the baby's feed, and we shan't go far after that."

With babies you have to give in. The sun was beginning

to drop, and Mark was feeling the need of this very mournful ditty as the pleasant summer trees went by, and cattle and sheep, and the Moonbi Hills, the continual shriek and flash of parrots off the road, and every few hundred yards a kestrel pinned beautifully against the sky. He sang,

'He reminds me of the wintertime,
   And of the summer, too,
And the many, many times I have held her in my arms
  Just to keep her from the foggy, foggy dew.'

And the dew began to fall in the Upper Hunter Valley, and they looked for a place, with decent shelter for pretty faces, all one way or another cut up. They found it by Page's River, below Murrurundi.

Murrurundi lies below the Liverpool Range, stinking hot in summer, but they were early in the season and the night was cool. They woke to the sight of the high tops wrapping them around, catching the first of the light like a solemn band in the distance, with drums and trumpets, but just beyond hearing. Oh, Lord, how musical the hills are, and the line of the hills against the sky, and passing clouds. You wake up early in the open, and it's a fine thing. Besides, the two boys had slept under one of Corrie's blankets, each, and they woke cold.

"Get moving, Par," Mark shouted, persecuting him to prevent this urge to prayer and poetry at sunset and dawn. You can't afford it in a secular society, especially with alfresco plumbing. "Par, Par, time to sit on your pottie."

What made Mark so urgent was to see Lin curled up on the bank inside his sleeping-bag, with shoots of unconsidering auburn hair spilt out on the green meadow. It's a risky thing to catch a girl sleeping, especially if you were friendly with her before, and she's in your sleeping-bag. He could easily see how the gods of the streams and woodland got so randy sometimes. But Lin sat up in a shower of her hair and said,

"Must boil Jacky's milk."

Jacqueline was what Corrie said the name was, and it needed a very good glue for a name like that to stick to a small baby, when you knew the things it did. Though afterwards girls wear it well enough.

"I'll go to the farm for some."

When he got back he helped Par with boiling the water. Biddy had dozed in the car, and she had a headache, but moving about began to help it. When you bed down in the city night by night, you don't know anything about the sum of human ailments, but out by Page's River there's only a kind of a hedge privacy. Soon they were belting along, and Mark was driving the Volksy.

A proper man ought to be ambitious about small things. Here was Lin beside him and the baby in the back, and it was what he wanted, well enough. The others had seen it coming. They had tried not to show.

"Can't you sit a little closer?"

"No," said Lin, but doing it. "We're elderly, we've got a baby in the back seat."

"Yes, but not ours."

"Oh, but it might have to be," Lin said.

"Why, but, Lin, you'll have me then?"

"I was only joking."

But she put both hands on his left knee and drew a long breath. She remembered his kisses the night before. She'd fain be persuaded. That sleeping-bag, he said, was a king-size engagement ring. And then he said there was risk in sleeping without a roof on. You had to be protected from the sky.

"Cheer up," Lin said, "it may never happen."

She might have been giving herself advice, and that's a sad happiness.

"Why ever—"

"Mark," said Lin, inclined to give him back his knee, "I'm nearly twenty-two."

"Yes," he said, "I know. Quite ripe."

But she wouldn't smile.

"It's bad for a girl to be older than her man. She ages quicker."

"Oh, it'll come at us very slowly," he said. He couldn't bear being fifty, just then.

"It's important, though," Lin said, with her back on the door, taking her pleasure in the look of him, without disguise. And it was trusting.

"The thing is, honey," and he sought her knee, "that we're young now, and when there's just the pair of us we share each other's ages. Increase and multiply. And what's a year to you and me?"

"You've still got to meet my mum. You've taken Corrie on the chin, but you won't take her."

"Oh, well, I haven't got to. She's not in the treaty."

"Families should be, all the same."

"There's a bit of it in the back seat, then."

"Yes, that's true. You don't mind lending a hand, do you?"

She was offering to put her head on his shoulder, but she sat up, cured.

"I almost forgot. You're a dangerous driver."

"I think I'm improving."

She laughed. "All over, I think you are. Though I'm glad you were once."

"Once what?"

"Dangerous."

They changed drivers and the baby woke and Mark

found himself nursing and singing *Oh, oh, Antonio*, a thing not very likely when he set out with Biddy. Of course Lin said he had a nice singing voice and got him singing more. They're clever, women, they understand vanity, and when to bring it on. Besides, it's fun to be humored in your weaknesses, by your girl friend, and to show her that she can go on doing it, and that you see through it nicely, thank you.

Only the baby seemed to take no notice, but she got bored at last, and fell asleep.

"She won't sleep long," said Lin, "she's hungry."

"Where are all the others?"

"Behind us. Do you care?"

"Oh, no."

21

"I'll do the op in February, when she's three months old," the surgeon said. "Late February should suit very well,"

Lin looked over at Corrie, filled with a huge relief. Only a few months of babyhood for them to bear, and then that little face would only be ruined by scars getting better. Everybody would see they'd be getting better, and they wouldn't feel like criticizing. Jacky herself would never know about it. She'd never have to bear the derision of her schoolmates, and to live her whole life alone, watch others in their happiness. Lin could have danced a pirouette. She could have hugged them all there and then. People were kind, and oh wouldn't Biddy be pleased? Mark, too, perhaps. They'd both gone home.

"And what I'll do," said the surgeon, "is this. I'll cut with the lines of the mouth, as far as there are any. She'll have a nice little mouth, I can promise you that. Then there's these warts beside the ears. Quite simple. I'll excise them, stitch up, and the marks will go, completely. No worry. This growth on the cheek could be troublesome, yes. If there's a vein connecting it with the ear, then the cut will be much bigger. I must warn you it could be across the cheek. You see, it all happened (we know that much) at the same time in pregnancy. I don't need to tell you that these malformations are related, do I? Did you ever take drugs, Ms. Jamieson, for instance?"

"Yes, pot," said Corrie quickly, "or I think it was pot. Three times, maybe, of a weekend, for kicks, you know. Mike stopped me."

The surgeon didn't want to go on with that. "Well," he said, "it's past. And the baby's bottle-fed, you tell me?"

"Yes, completely."

"If there's no connecting vein, we'll cut that lot out in the middle of the cheek, and the cut will travel down over the jaw as she grows, and vanish into the rest of her life. What you've got to understand is that I can't put back the body of gristle that's missing. The cheeks won't be equal. I could pack the left cheek, but it wouldn't do, for the other one will grow differently. It's when she's twelve or so, and a pretty girl, that she'll have to decide for herself. Whether to have it packed or not."

"Will she—Will they be very different?" Lin asked. "I mean, like the moon on the wane?"

The surgeon smiled to reassure them.

"Everybody's cheeks are different. And we have to put up with them, like our character in our faces. Even your good looks aren't symmetrical, you know, or you'd part your hair in the middle, for a start. Think how squint most noses are. She'll be as normal as the next girl, you see, so don't worry. It's an anxious prospect for you, that's all."

"Oh, thank you, Dr. Pretherick. You've been such a help already. And so patient with us. Please forgive us. It's such a help even to see that you know about it all."

"In February then," said Dr. Pretherick. "The 25th. That's really all, except for one thing, and I must ask. It's too important. Have you thought what's going to happen to this baby? I'm not just curious."

"Yes," said Corrie at once. "It's my baby. I'm keeping it, of course."

"I see," said Dr. Pretherick. "That'll be all then. February 25th, at three o'clock. The op will be next day."

They came away, in silence, through the long corridors, thinking of this end to the consultation. When they were in the open air Lin said, first of all,

"That's fine then. Aren't you pleased?"

"No," said Corrie, "I'm not. What business was it of his, who keeps the baby?"

"I don't think he was too pleased with your answer, either, was he?"

"Well, she's mine, and he'd best not do anything about it. Do the op and that's all. That's all we're asking him. He'll want a pretty bill for it, I bet you, and when it's paid the transaction's over. We're rid of him."

"And who pays? How'll you pay?"

"God knows," Corrie said. "It isn't February yet. You get months, and even years, to pay for a fridge or a house, don't you? So why not for a new cheek? Is the car locked? I'm done in with all that."

"Yes, let's get home for a cup of tea."

But the doctor had raised a main question, that couldn't be let slip or set aside. In a real sense they all were victims of

Corrie's behavior, and dependent on it, whatever it might be. It's all right calling for permissiveness, if you mean to put up with the result. But the permissives never seem to. By definition, they walk away, and Lin knew it. Yet Jacky was one of the facts of her life, too, now.

"We could abandon her, of course," said Mark, one Saturday morning in January, in Lin's place.

Mark had got a job as a bricklayer's helper, and was making a lot of money and getting his back red by wheeling bricks to the hoist on a new block of apartments to devastate the landscape of Artarmon. It made him feel responsible, a pillar of the work force, fit to swill with the mob at half past four, if he hadn't invented an excuse. In training, he said he was, and they respected that. Among the boys you can sacrifice anything for sport, but anything, even your daily intake of beer. He went home and ran two miles through paths in the bush and thought how comical brickies were, and counted up the money he'd need in his last year at the university, and felt tough all over with trade unionism. You get it somewhere in the gut, and it spreads. No sentiment in the building trade, was what they told him. Before December was out, he'd recovered the cost of the Volksy smash. He didn't speak about it, but he hoped it wasn't too mean to tot it up. And now there was this kid to mend and Corrie would have no money. It would all come back on Lin. So, hell why should they do it? It wasn't their business: nor was any of the fun. Send bloody Mike the bill at last.

"Of course we could abandon her," he said again, quite fiercely.

Par was there from Newcastle, enjoying his Saturday excursion. He sat there, trying to look as if he'd just heard an ordinary saying, or Mark's usual bold talk. Corrie was out buying something. Lin was moving around, and the remark was meant for her. She didn't fire up, for violence is to be expected now and means less in its targets than the misery it causes, far less. That's why it's so pernicious.

"I think," said Lin, "it's just what the doctor feared we might do."

"Correct," said Mark. "And you know what? He was dead right."

"Would *you* abandon her?"

"Question hardly makes sense. Like asking me if I'd abandon a nuclear station, if it was left me. I couldn't look after it, and that's all."

"The thing is," Par said, "I think she should get married."

"That's what she thinks, too," said Mark, "but who's to marry her, tell me that?"

"Would you abandon Jacky?" Lin persisted, excluding everything but Mark.

"What d'you want me to say? Truth, or romance?" He thought of his bankbook and the money he had in it, but how could he mention that? He'd pay a bit of that op, he knew that now. Now that there was money to be had, students helped their mates, or some did. He was angry at her for doubting him, even though he'd flung out that remark. It was funny how they squabbled about this.

"I'd just like to say this," Lin said quietly, "before Corrie comes back. That baby isn't mine and I'm not pining for it, but I know I'm gonna be left with it, and I'll just have to keep it like the nose on my face, and like it, too. 'Cos I'm the nearest to it in the end. So goodbye, Mark boy, or get used to that."

"Oh, how d'you mean? They mightn't let you. Corrie mightn't let you. The state mightn't let you. What are you going on about?"

"All right, off you go. I know all that—"

"What does Biddy think?" Par blurted out, not liking private rows.

Mark was glad of the chance. "Biddy thinks it'd be best to be adopted."

"I know that, too. But it's all wound up with women, and this face. You can surely see, if we've got to nurse it to this op, and it's not till late February till it happens, that we can't think to give it away then, poor thing. It's not like rearing tomatoes for sale."

"I know," said Mark. Everybody was so eager to show that they knew, but Lin chipped in again.

"You can see, can't you? Can't you see how we've all got to screw our minds up to this date in February and this that we have to do, and love her, just love her, right up to there and past it?" Lin then burst into tears. "Poor Jacky, poor kid. At the mercy of us all."

Mark was abashed.

"I know, I know," he said again. "I was just being sour, that's all. You'll see who'll help and who won't. And I'll help," he said, "all you want, and as long."

He got up and made toward Lin, but thought better of it, walked about in an agitated way, snapping his fingers.

"I'm sorry," he said. "Because you'll be left, we'll be left, of course I see that."

Lin began to look at him over her shoulder and between her fingers, better pleased, a smile beginning.

"Will you please stop that snapping, for heaven's sake?"

"Yes," Mark said, "I will. Oh, like a beer, Par? I mean, let's all have coffee, shall we? Anything. I'll make it."

22

They took Jacky to see Biddy, and every time there was something lying waiting for the baby. They always tried it on, stood back, pretended not to see the shocking little lip, and then their eyes would question each other.

"There's nothing wrong with her," Mark would say. But men are reckless.

Yet there she was, crawling and climbing on Lin's shoulder with wind to get rid of, and Lin would look down expecting it, giving herself a double chin, just like a real young mother, delighted. And to see Lin then, in Biddy's house, made Mark reach for Jacky's hand, the touch of human flesh. He thought he saw Jacky's eyes come over with happiness, too, creeping there on Lin's shoulder, biting into it, screwing up her nose, watching him, intelligent.

Once Biddy greeted them with, "I've been thinking. You ought to go and see your mum."

"That's what I've been thinking."

From the way Lin agreed, they could see that it wasn't quite on.

"I know you're frightened of it. But this op, Lin, it's bound to cost money. And Corrie's not got insurance. Hasn't a bean, and never will have. And your step-father's a professor, after all." Biddy paused, eloquently. "Besides, they'll want to know. Whether it's a boy or a girl, I mean."

"They've shown no sign."

But they were away at a conference in Singapore, and it

130

was late January before Mark and Lin could visit at their house. They sat in the living room, and drank tea, and heard about the conference.

"Ah, you should have seen. The exhilaration of it, my dear. I wish you could have come, thought of you many times."

"Yes, but how could I, Mum?"

"Well, just the thing for your reporting, you know that? Your father would have—you know?—delighted in it. Reg got so much out of it. New ideas, latest research, such very valuable contacts my dear you can't think. Scholars of international repute, world figures—Jacobinski was there."

"Oh—"

"Gretchen *liebchen*, they don't—"

"And you know, Lin darling, they talk just like ordinary men, what do you think? But isn't it very chic? Get drunk, eat too much, have affairs, too, are completely sold on Women's Lib, completely, I assure you. One of them said to me, you know—he said, 'You know, Gretchen.' They called me Gretchen, of course. 'You know, Gretchen,' he said, oh, so coyly, 'colleagues at work means colleagues in bed.' So knowledgeable he was! I laughed so much they all looked over. 'At least I know that,' I said. And he roared with laughter. Didn't care for his huge reputation. I was so amused. But it was too hot in Singapore, but much too hot. It's not the place for love. Too canned, with air conditioning. Philosophers are made like other men. But what have you been doing all this time I've been expecting you to call, I must say."

A certain sprightliness there was, European on the run, even Viennese, like a lady not quite extricated from the opera, but flourishing nonetheless. She wasn't interested in them. Mark would rather have had the Queen of the Bikies by a long way. Because, if you had to be, it was better to be blatant without any thin veneer. And this one was matronly as well. Ruled out of her conversation, Mark began to wonder what happened when the doors were closed and the professor had to hear it all in his own house. Ah, well, he'd asked for it. He probably was impudent in German, in reply.

They didn't rouse themselves at all when Jacky was mentioned, at last. Corrie had said they wouldn't, and had refused to come. It was just as well they didn't bring the baby. Sitting there, so full of indignation at the kettledrum she was, Mark began to wriggle and then to think he'd never be there again and then to speak his mind,

"For God's sake, world figures, lech and preach and peck, and you leave your own daughter struggling with all this. Terrific bloody boozeup, telling us. You've got a grand-daughter you didn't want, how's that? You're a grand-mother now, and time to talk sense. She needs help, does little Jacky. We've got us, and we've got the surgeon on our side, but what about you? You gonna do anything? For a hare-lip, or next thing to it?"

The prof got up and left the room, and Mark got up.

"Sorry," he said, "I shouldn't have said that, but surely you should know. And for a girl. We're doing all—"

The next thing he felt was a sharp slap across his face.

"Get out of here, you! Who are you, how dare you?"

She was pointing and pushing him, and her breasts were very furious. Wait, but wait a minute. Mark was trying to collect himself, and to get at something still on his mind, shamed as he was and all. At last it came to him.

"It's all right to do these insults," Mark said, as he rattled the floor, "but not to speak them."

"No, it's not. Get out! You mustn't date my daughter. I'll not have it. I forbid it, Lin! I'm furious to have him in this house. No, not a word. Insult my husband."

She was still talking, after she had slammed the door on him.

"Professor Croll is a distinguished man, world man, and knows how to behave. And who is he? Crummy Aussie *dummkopf, schweinhund*. What will you do, dear? Yes, better go, too. Goodbye."

They stood on the garden steps, among the neglected camellia trees, made their way down the path and out at the gate, still hearing the foreign voice sometimes, wild with its opportunity of virtue.

"Well, that's that." Lin was in the driving seat. "I knew we shouldn't have come, and what a fool I was to bring you."

"I'm sorry, Lin, I blew my top. Sitting listening to her little world. And not even my affair."

"It was," said Lin, edging over to his side. "Just let me come to, will you? Mum's—Mum's been abusing us all our lives, and she's never had it as hard as that. She deserved it all."

She lay with her head on his shoulder, staring out.

"I knew you wouldn't get on with Mum. Or him. It's stunning, but I'm very glad."

"Sure they were mean and selfish—"

"And what I thought was, you might take a look and run away—"

"They won't give you a penny, that lot. God, it's hateful."

"—and leave me."

"All expenses paid to Singpore."

"And here you haven't left me, Mark. Which cheek was it?"

She was stroking the convenient one.

"While we were hitching to Lazarus and back, out of our abundance."

"Which cheek?" She kissed him. "Was it that one?"

"They're sitting pretty. And he's nicely resigned to it. This one," he said, squeezing her till she cried for help. And then again.

After that, he worked overtime twice or thrice a week, for expiation. But when Corrie heard of their visit to the Crolls, and of its ill-success, she was very depressed. It wasn't that she cried or carried on, but sometimes when she was feeding the baby a tear would come in her eye and down her cheek until it grew cold and she wiped it away and dried her finger on her dress, and started again. She hadn't meant any of this when she went to live with Mike more than six months ago, when the baby couldn't be shifted and she knew for sure there would be one. She thought, then, that Mike would marry her, that it was the obvious thing to do. But he hadn't. She thought that she was following her mother's style, and that it lasted without upsets. True, from time to time her mother had been angry, and even beside herself, but it had always been at them, her children, or her husband. Other men she seemed to manage with queenly unconcern. But it hadn't been so for Corrie, somehow, and here her mother was no help, was callous. February now loomed very near.

"Callous, what else? What could you expect," Mark had said, "with that recipe for love? It only amounts to shoving people off."

But he had caught a tartar in her mum. Corrie didn't like Mark, who paid her no attention at all, except for home-truths, and she was very wearied of sitting there waiting, on the shelf at seventeen. Oh, it was all very well to watch him smoodging up to Lin, and she could have taken it in better days, with men of her own, and older than Mark was, so callow and new at it, no hair on his face for all his cleverness. From what they told her it was Mark that upset the visit to her mum's. Though Corrie had refused to go herself, in desperation she must have held on to the hope that they'd come around. Her own mother, after all, and this was real trouble. And yet, there was all that stuff about her doorstep, and how they'd be strewn on it, babies and all. Corrie was ironing, dragging it out. Lin couldn't have liked going, but she swallowed her pride.

And so Corrie's speculations went on. She named her friends over and over, all absent ones, and she thought where she had gone wrong, and of the boy friend at Cessnock that loved her first, when she was still at school, scheming and trusting both. Perhaps he was the one to help her, he was nice? Anything was better than this, just waiting, just depending, like a stray cat, or one of those refugees from Bangladesh. Lin was meaning to take over the child, she could see that, and then Corrie would be out, hunting up work on her own. She didn't fancy working in the city.

The more she sat and thought, the more was the urge to do something, till one day Lin came back and Corrie wasn't there, nor the baby either. It was afternoon, and Lin thought nothing at first. She'd be walking, or shopping. But then she didn't come home, and Lin looked and found the child's things were gone, and a suitcase.

She phoned Mark.

23

"I tell you," Lin said, "it puts Jacky at risk, wherever Corrie is. She mightn't be fit for her op."

Mark had been showing some cynical relief. He came into the city soon enough when Lin phoned him, but not without an exasperated glee. His own view of Corrie was confirmed: that she was dangerous, that you couldn't rely on her: but he was also glad to be free of those sudden heavy responsibilities of being middle-aged, with a child on your hands, and it somebody else's. Good luck to her, he said. Let her be where she is, so long as it isn't in Lin's apartment. There isn't room for her and me.

But Lin was mad at him.

"Think I'm doing this for fun? Think *you'd* like to have a mouth and a half? To live your life with? Oh, come off it."

"But I suppose she still *means* to turn up at the hospital for the op?"

"I suppose so, at the back of her mind, maybe. But it can't be why she beetled off. If she meant to turn up at the hospital, she only had to stay here. We all meant that."

"She's a fool. Oh, I can't tell what goes on in her flimsy mind. You can't trust her with herself, far less with her own baby. She must have gone looking for a man."

Mark expected Lin to be wild at a taunt like that. He meant her to be, but to his surprise she agreed with him.

"That's what I think, and I want your help, please, Mark."

"Oh, anything."

"What's today? Wednesday. I want you to come to Armidale at the weekend."

"Oh, but that's okay. Eloping, are we? Let's go, for sure."

"I'm quite serious. And I've only you to turn to. Course, I could go myself."

"I'll go," Mark said. "But why?"

"I've been thinking. We've got till Friday to hear from her, and if so it's off."

"Oh, no. Couldn't we just go for kicks, then?"

"Stop fooling. She'll seek out her old haunts, I think. Might go to plead with Mike, even."

136

"God, but that'd be useless. She knows there's another woman."

"Yes, but there's a kind of a commune, you bet. They've got to encourage each other. Might be some other guy ripe for a switch."

"I see. Cynical, eh? Let joy be unconfined. Hope he likes kids."

"I don't think she has a hope," Lin said, "but, poor Corrie, she's gone."

"Think we should tell the police? She might be at the bottom of the harbor, baby and all."

Lin wasn't to be flustered by that.

"No," she said, "that's not Corrie. And I don't want to put the police on to her. You can—you can start something. She might get used to them, and there's the street."

"What's the difference?" Mark said, viciously, for boys have little mercy on the Corries they meet, and less on the Corries they make. Just think of Mike.

But Lin took it gently.

"I know," she said, "but there is a difference, and we've all got to cling to it."

They got off on Friday after work, and still no news of Corrie. Once, as they drove along, Mark said,

"I'm not caring about Corrie yet. I'm not for retrieving her all my life. It's only for you and Jacky that I'm doing this, you know."

"Of course, I know. So long as it draws you in. Just don't be half-hearted, will you?"

"Oh, well we could just go up the coast," Mark said. "We're not gonna find her. Australia's too big, and we could have a bonza weekend."

He drew onto the verge.

"Time for a bit of loving. But can't we have a cuddle, Lin?"

Lin looked at her watch, and that was quite an answer in itself.

"We're not at Newcastle yet, nor near it."

"Oh, couldn't we—?"

"Too nervous," she said. "Can't be at peace."

"Are we going to stay the night at Par's place?"

Lin had insisted on calling up Par on Thursday, and he was expecting them. The sister of a girl like Corrie, Lin said, had better watch what she's about. Besides, Par's mother deserved to know what was coming. And there was another reason. Par's family were milkmen. They turned in early, they got up early. Lin and Mark could be on their road to Armidale by four in the morning, easily. And Par could even come. It was Saturday, and his father did the round. Dad's turn Saturdays and Sundays, that was practically the whole trade union side of it: no strikes, no nothing, Par said.

Mark, for his part, was hankering after the bright stars of the country, and his sleeping-bag, and what he called a practice with Lin in hers beside him. Nothing but the two of them, and the universe at arm's length. But she was not to be diverted. Perhaps it would have to wait till Saturday night, if he killed Par off, first? Anyway, they made for Par's.

In phoning him, Lin had asked Par to take a run to Cessnock if he could, to inquire after Corrie there. The Jamiesons had lived in Cessnock, when her Dad sang in the garden that he cared for nobody. Corrie had begun her ventures there, and there were children now entering school, not hers, but belonging to her consequently married friends, and Lin's. Maybe now Corrie would be showing them her own child, and how she was up to these deeds herself.

"Not very likely," Mark said, when he was told.

"No, but she had friends. She might think she could fall back on them. Sue Lake, Jenny Paton."

"Oh, girls, you think?"

"No, Possum, too."

"Who's Possum?"

"One of her boy friends. I can't tell where Corrie's gone."

That conversation, like all the others, petered out. Par, being a docile chap, went to Cessnock, and found no news of Corrie. Yes, he said, he'd talked to Sue Lake. And Jenny Paton. Possum wasn't there, they said.

"But where was he, where was he, Par?"

They didn't know where Possum was. Last thing they knew he was jackerooing.

"Oh, then to hell with Possum," said Mark. "He's nothing more than a name in the paper that you could find out with a pin. Has nothing to do with this."

"No," said Lin, lamely, "suppose not. But who has?"

Suddenly Lin broke down in front of them and Par's mother came and took her away and they stirred like mangy tigers in a cage, sat down, got up, nibbled at grapes in a dish.

"Your fault that," Par said. "You're too impatient."

"Par, Par," said Mark, "maybe I am too impatient, yes, but what's it all about? And what are we to do?"

"Dunno," Par said. "She's maybe still in Sydney, I should think."

"But where would she go? She knows nobody there. Gee, Par, impatient or not, we've done a lot. We've done a lot, Par, and you get pretty sick of it when it's all thrown away. The baby was well, and Lin and Biddy watched things, and the surgeon was okay for February, and we—why, we went to see Professor Croll, even: a thing you wouldn't do lightly. We were all saving up for little Jacky, still are. You don't like a kid to have a mouth like that, now do you, Par?"

"No, by gee," said Par, not choosing his words. "I was counting I could put something in, too, maybe, if you had of let me?"

"You can't, Par. You can't now. They've gone to hell."

"Oh, no," said Par, softly.

"Well, maybe not to hell, but they won't be in Armidale any more than in Cessnock. You'll see."

"I took you to Armidale, once."

"Meaning what? Oh, I know, I know. When you didn't need to, you mean? I'll go. I'm perfectly willing. To do this for Lin. It's just that—a bloke gets desperate. When he's useless, Par? Please, please don't blame me."

"I don't," Par said. "Think you're a good guy, for a silvertail."

"Silvertail?"

"Well, you're a student, ain't you? They all got fortunes."

"I'm a brickie these days, Par. And glad to be. You better come to Armidale. You're off tomorrow."

"What, and play gooseberry? It'd be worse than the bikies' do."

"No, but it wouldn't. Fact is, we need you, Par. It'll keep us sweet. Funny thing, but we like our friends. Ask Lin."

They went to Armidale, came back again. Three of them in one car, driving in turns. And Corrie wasn't there. Mark drove them over to Mike's place to have a row with him and there was a girl taking washing off the line, with clothes-pegs on her dress and one between her teeth. She noticed them, hesitated, did everything more slowly. She knew they were some awkward business connected with her. She glanced toward the apartment, but didn't call. Quite nice-looking, slim, with the loom of youth. Too good for skivvy-ing, or for a sly-boots like this Mike.

"Oh, what's the use?" said Mark, ramming the gear into reverse and backing out, too quickly.

"Take care," Lin said. "No hurry."

She was in the back of the car, leaning forward, and her hair and head got in the way of Mark's hair and head as he looked behind him, but she didn't get out of his way. Instead, she smoodged among his hair. He took her hand, as it lay on the front seat.

"I'm sorry," he said. "It was the wrong thing again, and you two told me it was. I'm sorry. Let's go home."

Lin put her other arm around his neck, said nothing, was sad. Not even the hospital was able to tell them anything. You get there and you know it's no good asking anybody. Matron was kind, tried not to look vexed, made a note of Lin's working address.

24

You get that you might have had summer enough. You think at first that everything is made for the coast and the big waves and sunshine pouring down. The road beats with trucks, bikes, campers, and all. A paradise, that's what they're making for. And they make no sign as they pass, but you know they're bursting fit, hair done, necks swarthy with body hair leaping up at their throats, not a collar and tie among them, suntanned already. There couldn't be a care in all that mob of the blessed. But couldn't there?

Ten weeks ago Mark had set out with nothing but the flimsiest of jeans wrapped around his bankbook and his legs, and look what he'd copped out now. A bikie, a Biddy, a woman and her sister and her stray kid, and all of them, but all of them, just slipping through his fingers with the summer, petering into undetermined troubles. Come the beginning of March and time for term again, and you might as well have spent the summer at your books, or better, far better. At least you could take them with you, indwelling, a part of yourself for the rest of your days.

Funny thing, though. Not many people seemed really to like it that way, not so as to act properly upon it. Even the prof and his wife preferred Singapore and contacts, and just passing the time. Anything to make life go, so long as it was selfish. And here they were beneath the stars at Murrurundi for the second time—him, Par, and Lin—and none the better for all their journeys. He listened to the other two sleeping very peacefully, so that he had to stop his thinking to hear their breathing. Lin was sound as sound, her life sunk into the cage of her ribs, and, suddenly, it filled him with wonder and tenderness to have her so comfortably there with them, with him, long after midnight and through the rest of the night and not thinking it particularly odd. It wasn't useless after all.

I'm loving you, girl, he thought, and that's maybe summer enough.

"Par," he cried, "but Par? I've got to ask you, man. Will you be best man for us, Par? Par, please, you hear me. It's not a thing that can wait. We'd like it above all things."

Par's breathing stopped. And Lin's. They were wide awake, and still.

"Is it happening now?" Par said.

"No, not just yet awhile."

"Because, if so," Par said, "I'm gonna heat a red-hot stick, that's all. And you'll bloody get it anyhow if you wake me like that again. There's mosquitoes," Par said, "why didn't you tell me? Where's the repellent?"

They'd brought a net this time, and rigged it up on a low branch, as good as a tent. You get one or two mosquitoes for company, nonetheless: and if one swallow doesn't make a summer, one mosquito mars it very well. Still, they're better than ants, in bed.

"Hell," Par said, "I'll have to go for a walk now, thanks to you. Yes, I'll be your best man, sure. If it's on a Friday or a Saturday."

He was out by this time, feeling better already, calling like Satan across the hollow deep of Hell. Mark anxiously tried to cut him out.

"Thanks. Just don't give us a toaster for a wedding present, will you? I've had enough of that. And stand further away. There's ladies present and it makes me nervous."

Lin just let them talk. But Mark had found her hand.

"It doesn't matter where Corrie is, does it?"

"Oh, yes, but it does." Her throat was too dry to talk. She stretched. "I was so sound asleep, and now my bones are aching, aching. Lend me your pillow, will you, for my hipbone?"

"Yes, if I can still sleep on it."

Mark had an arrangement of his clothes for a pillow, that was all.

"No fear you don't. And why did you wake us up, anyway, you boob?"

"I was miserable," Mark said, "but now it's gone."

"May I come in?" said Par, politely. "It's not easy, being a gooseberry in the night."

"Oh, I don't know. It's a fine world with you two," Lin said, turning over. "Makes me quite content."

"Yes," said Mark, "I know that, but you can only have the one of us, and that's me."

"At least I'm glad we came."

"Make yourself easy," Mark said.

"Still, I'm glad, too, that you're here, Par," said Lin, as they settled. "Extricates me, somehow."

They couldn't help discovering a certain happiness

around about them, a feeling that the world was the better for men and women. They fell asleep again.

Or the boys did, and it was Lin's turn to lie awake, alerted by Mark's half-jocular demonstrations, till the whole of her life began to pass cheerless before her and on into the uncomforting future. It was of no purpose to have someone to marry then, but to have her sister, and her father, and especially her sister's child, this Jacky, so defenseless. Growing up for them had been a species of robbing one another, and it began early. Here was Jacky, already at three months on a life adrift, left to the freaks and chances of her relatives. Corrie could be anywhere. She wouldn't let so slight a thing as a baby bar her out of the life she wanted to live. Oh, she'd be decent enough, but only in the press of what she was intent on doing. What if there was, most likely, some new man? Or if she were abasing herself before her former lovers, one by one, and finding harsher things about them than the schoolgirl knew? And Corrie was only a schoolgirl even yet. And what if she were ill? Or in despair?

In the bleak dark beyond midnight, anything is true. Lin forgot to think that, however likely these things were, and indeed she was right more than once, one catastrophe would exclude the other, and she need not fear them all. But she did, and the night passed and she watched the dawn come and she was white and drained of other feeling. Except that she didn't want to hear any more bright nonsense from Mark.

Mark saw how white she was, and it upset him.

"Par," he said, as they boiled the water, "what's wrong with her?"

"Don't know," said Par, not looking.

"You've noticed then? Stop whistling, will you, and tell me?"

"Yip," said Par.

"Well? And what else?"

You could go on asking Par. Native politeness made him always answer, instead of asking you back, or bawling you out. He was earnestly trying to see if the pot would ever boil.

"I'd say," said Par, "she's done in, that's all. She's game, but it's a long hike, for a bird. And it's rough, out here in the dew."

"Tell you what, Par, you're wrong, son. Hunting a family up, that's what does it. Raking them out of the past, like embers, still smouldering away, and not up to much. And now this infant. And bloody Corrie—"

"You're not to say that," Par said. "Doesn't help. Just take her this mug of tea, will you, and don't say nothing. Say I wouldn't let you, mind?"

He raised his voice for those last things, turning and waving to Lin, as Mark balanced the tea. Then Par turned to the fire and resumed his whistling, gingering the flames, sipping his noisy mug of tea. He had a native courtesy, had Par.

And Mark sat near Lin and never took his eye off her, watching for a chance to smile. She sipped at her tea, and sighed, and said,

"Oh, dear, that's better. What a night. As though I'd been wrung by devils."

"It'll be all right, it'll come good. There's a verse of Longfellow I remember now. Cheer up.

> 'And the night shall be filled with music
> And the cares that infest the day
> Shall fold up their tents like the Arabs
> And silently steal away.' "

"That's beaut," said Lin, smiling, "only it will never happen."

"Can't promise you it all, sweetheart, but . . . why, much

of it is happening. Now. We'll see to you, Par and me. Just drink your tea. It's egg and sausage for breakfast."

"Oh, couldn't face it. You two boys, you're kind to me."

"Sure. We'll be about all day, too."

"But I feel so—" Sad she was going to say, but she said, "—useless. I feel like Richard the Second, if it comes to poetry. Richard coming back and sure of trouble. *Feel want, taste grief, need friends.* Oh, Lord," said Lin, "with a family like mine. D'you think it's worth this trouble? Mark, d'you think a family should stick together, I mean? That it matters all that much?"

"Of course I do," he said. "Any family's worth it."

"Even my family?"

"Even yours, even Corrie, even a scratch family like us. It's not just for kindness that we're here. It's because—well, because you're our kind. We've picked you out. And as for a real family, it's the women that take the trouble, mostly. And draw men after, you know."

"Even after Corrie," said Lin. "But, oh, where is she? It makes you hard of heart, if you deliberately push them all away. I'm glad you don't want to, either. For I'm not to do that, not even to Mum. I'll go and see her again, after this is over. And Dad'll always be pleased to see me. He'd help now, if I could get at him, I'm sure."

Mark didn't put much trust in anybody who would only help his children if they could find him: but he was divorced, maybe that was the snag.

"Your tea cold? Let me get you some more. Poor Lin, I'm not much good at looking after girls, am I? Still, with practice. Come on, Par, what you up to? Come and talk. Made that breakfast yet?"

25

On Monday, when she was back at work, Lin had a call from Armidale, and it was Matron.

"I could have asked them to ring you," Matron said, "at the Sydney end, but maybe they wouldn't have got around to it."

"What is it, Matron?"

"Your sister is in the Women's Hospital, and you could go and see her."

"What's wrong? And why didn't she tell me? And where's Jacky?"

"Oh, Jacky's there," said Matron, and paused. "Perhaps you'd better call and see."

"I will, Matron, at once. Thanks very much. It was so kind of you to think of me."

"Oh," said Matron, "it's nothing. The least I could do. I was worried about that baby, like you. I know you've done plenty, as well. They say the baby's in very good shape and I'm giving you credit for that. She wouldn't have managed without you. And—are you there?—just don't be too upset. It'll all work out now, you'll see, bless you. Got it? Women's Hospital. Goodbye."

She hasn't told me which part of it, thought Lin, holding out the phone and looking at it.

"Goodbye" she said, reluctantly. "Thank you, Matron, thank you."

But Matron had receded into Armidale.

When Lin asked at the Inquiry Desk for Miss Jamieson

with the baby Jacqueline, they passed her on once or twice, but at last she got to Corrie, who was waiting for her, smoothing the sheet as Lin came in.

"Hullo," she said, "I'm pleased you've come."

Lin stood by the bedside, with a sister's half-accusing bedside manner after journeys here and there and other effort wasted.

"They came and asked me, a moment ago, if I had a sister. Had to describe you, Lin, tell them how beautiful you were."

Corrie looked up at her then. Tried smiling.

"Such a relief," she said, "to see you, really."

"But what's it all about?"

"I was going to ask them to get on to you today, I truly was."

"Brought you these grapes. Where's Jacky?"

"Jacky's all right. She's in another ward."

"Ward?"

"Well, nursery. There's nothing wrong with her."

"You don't mean the op's done then?"

"Oh, no, it isn't."

"Then why are you a patient? What's it for?"

"Nothing. I'm relieved about that, too. It's only gonorrhoea."

"Corrie! V.D.?"

"Yes, but—It's only gonorrhoea. They're letting me out, Mum's coming for me. Sister, don't take on. Couldn't stand it. I was scared stiff it would be syphilis, but it's not."

They just sat for a bit, with this indigestible lump between them.

"And how does Mum come into it?"

"Matron phoned her. Thought she would be better about this than you, Lin. She said she'd take me. She's been in once, Mum."

"But what a revol—"

Corrie shrugged. "Not a revolution. She's just the same. Told me she didn't want to do it, to have me. But Matron told her flat I couldn't stay here. I can't go on about it, churns me up, they're all bad to me. And they're keeping Jacky. Till the op."

"Oh," said Lin, "that's good, at least. They know what they are doing. Who did you catch this from?"

"Don't know. But maybe Mike. Suppose he has it, too. A lousy trick, that's all, for Nature to play."

Lin thought of the girl with the clothes-peg in her mouth, looking at them slowly through the windshield, then slowly pegging some garment up. It agitated Lin: so lovable an action, so nasty a thing to be in for.

"We went off to Armidale to look for you, last weekend."

"Whatever for? Who's we?"

"Mark, Par. Why didn't you tell me?"

"But I was worried stiff. I couldn't. And after Mum had thrown you out, I went to see Mar—this medical student I knew. Marge, a woman this time, Lin, aren't I good? And she brought me here, for observation."

"But a woman would have let me know—"

"You're smart, I must admit. There was a man in the first place, and he brought in Marge, and—"

"That's fine. Don't tell me any more. Are you happy here?"

"Oh, they look after me. I'm a specimen. I'll mend. And you aren't out of it long with gonorrhoea, there's that. And there's plenty of others here. Waifs of love like me. Besides, I tell you, Mum's coming, so you'd better hop it."

"I wonder if they'll let me see Jacky. Think I'll try. I'm glad I got you, Corrie. Don't run away again. Please not. You don't know how it hurts us."

There was no good ticking Corrie off. You had to hope

that V.D. would do that, and sharp unhappiness. And yet it seemed to make them ask for more. Drove them somehow through their own drab suffering world, the Oliver Twists of sex. And Mum would seize her chance, Lin knew that. Would look after her daughter in her high-spirited, shrill English, scolding all the time. It was easier than being virtuous herself. Soon they would separate for their mutual convenience, and Professor Croll's.

They let her see Jacky, though the nurses immediately called the Matron in. Very nicely, Matron stressed that with Lin's permission (which Matron knew was hardly necessary) they were keeping Jacky, and she'd have her operation in ten days' time.

"I'm sure you'll see the sense of that," Matron said, a little pointedly.

"I do," said Lin, humbly. "And I'm sorry we failed. We did try."

Matron, seeing a difference, quickly took Lin's arm and gripped it hard.

"You mustn't worry. Dr. Pretherick wants to know what he's got on his hands. We got in touch with him at once, when we saw the little face. He wants to be sure she'll be fit for this op. She's only a tiny baby. But she'll be very well seen to: like a princess, you're not to worry. Better wait now till after it's over, and then you can come as soon as you like, to the Children's Hospital, that is. You'll be very welcome, for the baby's sake. You've had a heavy load and you haven't deserved it."

Lin made her way out among the babies and the patients and the nurses, and never said hullo to Jacky. It made her feel near tears, and very old. That love should be entangled in this carelessness. It wasn't the sorrow that she minded, but the carelessness, the utter unconcern for the other bits of love. But then, that was it, there was a fatal unhappiness in Corrie's way, and it wasn't hard to see. So damp a prospect for a young girl's life.

Could she have prevented it herself, as Corrie's nearest friend in the world? It was no comfort to think not. It was no comfort to think so. But what else could she have done?

26

The term started again on the 5th of March, and on the night before Mark was talking to his mum. She knew a lot already, and she happened to be there, and somebody had to hear his review of the summer done.

"The kid's coming on, Mum. Took Lin this afternoon, and you wouldn't know how wonderful it is to see her with a little mouth. Of course, there's bandages, but the doc's pleased. Lin was upset again, but then so was I. You feel kind of thankful, for somebody so small, don't you? You know how many stitches?"

"No," said Mum, amused at him, but keeping to her ironing, as mums will, never looking up in the face of this new son of hers.

"Forty-two."

That stopped the ironing, though, and the amusement, too.

"The poor little mite. You think you could bring her up here one day, Mark? When she's out? I'd love to see her. Poor little Jacky."

"Oh, she isn't poor. She'll do well. She has brains, you'll

see. And one or two folk to be always rooting for her," Mark added, quietly. "Kids need that."

"Who'll look after her?"

"There's Corrie."

"And who pays the bill?"

"We'll all be having a go at that. Lin, Biddy, Par, and me. For the sake of the summer we had. Like to come in on it?"

"No, thanks. One from this family might be enough, don't you think?"

"Maybe so."

"And where will her home be?"

"Dunno. Mum, to tell the truth, I don't know *who'll* look after her. Wanted to ask you. It gives Lin little peace."

"But Lin would never get her, if that's what she's thinking. She's a single woman, and not her mother. They wouldn't have it."

"No, the state wouldn't, I know. Corrie might, though."

His mother shook her head. "That way," she said, "they'd be at Corrie's mercy. And Lin can't want it, can she? A young woman with a life of her own?"

"Well, Mum, I know this. Corrie's too uncertain to be a mum. She'll never be at home like you, the center of everything. She's caught. She couldn't afford to do that. She'd find herself with no place, again."

"At least it's lucky for her, not to be the center of everything. That's only hard work, that is."

"You wouldn't shift it, would you? . . . Mum?"

"Well, what is it, son?"

"One day, Mum, I'm going to marry Lin, if she'll have me."

"Have you asked her?"

"Yes."

"And what does she say?"

"She says she will."

It was a funny thing, but Mark had always thought that this would be unwelcome news, to be met with cautious dismay, and here it wasn't. His mum was bent to her work, but she did look up sharply at her son and then went on ironing interminably. It looked as though the conversation would stop.

"We haven't met this girl. Perhaps you should ask her up on Saturday."

"We were going to see Par, and Janey. Lin wants to see Janey. Janey'll be having a baby soon. Gee, I hope it's okay. You know, Mum, before this summer began, I didn't even know these things were serious. Thought they were just fun. You can be pretty raw, can't you? Arrogant, too, maybe. But what a fool! Must have been horrible for you?"

His mother wasn't saying anything, kept on at her work amazed, so he had to go on.

"Suppose we might go to Newcastle next week, just the same? But what'll Dad say? If I bring Lin up?"

"Oh, that. You can leave him to me. Just do as I say, will you? You won't be getting married yet awhile, will you?"

"No, not till I'm through at school: unless—"

"Unless what?"

"Unless, well, I don't know that Jacky's our problem, is she? But if we had to, we'd adopt her. And we'd get married then, so as to do it."

"You won't have to adopt her, I hope. It's not how people begin. Too out of the way."

"I know that, Mum, but if you knew Corrie, and Corrie's own Mum . . . Still, I suppose, they might make a go. Lin's been back to see her mother, and Corrie's living there, meantime. On side for the present, at least."

"So—"

"Beg pardon?"

"So there's nothing—Do you remember the connection

you once drew between the hare lip and the baby's mouth? That shocking suggestion? There was nothing in it, was there?"

"No," said Mark, steadily, "don't think there was."

"So you just insulted Professor Croll, that's all? Not to say Corrie, too?"

"Suppose I did, suppose maybe I must have. But I didn't insult them all that much."

"How can you say that?"

"They knew what they were at all the time, don't tell me. It wouldn't stand much looking into, would it? It's a short step from them to what I said."

"But the smugness of you! Uppitty as you are, you students. As if you were perfect yourself. Who makes you the judge?"

"They do, don't they? You can't just pretend they're doing nothing. You've got to decide for yourself, and whether you'll join them. I just happen to detest all those buggers in the cause of progress that don't give a damn for anything but their own sweet will. All right then, humbuggers then, for that's what they are. They'll cheat themselves, but they'll be free. That fellow's a professor, a light to lighten the young. And look how he does it. I'll not apologize to him. To Corrie, much rather. She's only seventeen."

"You get so vicious. It doesn't do you any credit, Mark, to go on like this."

"Nor does it do him any. What do we owe his sort? Nothing but the mess we're in. They're clever rogues, I see that well enough. There's always some like him, abusing academic freedom for their crafty ends. And they have the hide to think that students don't see, or if they see that they admire them. I doubt if Jacky will be any better in his hands than in ours, frankly. It's love she needs, not money. Ah, well, next summer, anyway, we'll be looking for our wave."

He rose to go to his room.

"Thanks, Mum, for listening: sorry if I sounded off. But that's our plan. I don't know why, but I always thought you might be a bit annoyed at it, and here you're not?"

"Annoyed? To hear that you're growing up? To hear of a good girl? Young men," she said, "are idle creatures, and it's the best protection they can get, a real nice girl. And these days, it seems, they might need it sooner than usual."

"She's real capable, I'll say that for her. And, you know this, she sleeps without snoring."

He was out of the room. Like jesting Pilate, he didn't stay for an answer to that.